IT WAS SWAMPY. . . .

I could smell the creek and feel the ground ooze beneath my feet. A rooflike structure supported by pilings stretched over the dark area. I listened to the lap of water against the pilings, then footsteps sounded above. Fear flashed through me like light off a knife blade.

I made my way forward into the shallow water—slowly, so as not to make a ripple of sound. I heard the light thump of feet on wet ground, then mud sucking back from shoes. My pursuer was close—whether male or female, I couldn't tell—the night was cloudy and the person's face and body covered. I hid behind one of the pilings.

I heard the person walking slowly, prowling and listening, prowling and listening. I guessed that only ten feet remained between us. If I moved, the person would know immediately where I was. But if I waited any longer, I might get trapped. . . .

Dark Secrets: Legacy of Lies
Dark Secrets: Don't Tell
Dark Secrets: No Time to Die

Available from Archway Paperbacks

DARK SECRETS
No Time to Die

Elizabeth Chandler

AN ARCHWAY PAPERBACK
Published by POCKET BOOKS
New York   London   Toronto   Sydney   Singapore

This book is a work of fiction. Names, characters, places and incidents are products of the author's imagination or are used fictitiously. Any resemblance to actual events or locales or persons, living or dead, is entirely coincidental.

AN ARCHWAY PAPERBACK *Original*

An Archway Paperback published by
POCKET BOOKS, a division of Simon & Schuster, Inc.
1230 Avenue of the Americas, New York, NY 10020

ISBN: 0-7434-0030-5

First Archway Paperback printing November 2001

10 9 8 7 6 5 4 3 2 1

DARK SECRETS is a trademark of Simon & Schuster, Inc.

AN ARCHWAY PAPERBACK and colophon are
registered trademarks of Simon & Schuster, Inc.

For information regarding special discounts for bulk purchases,
please contact Simon & Schuster Special Sales at 1-800-456-6798
or business@simonandschuster.com

Book design by Jaime Putorti
Front cover illustration by Sandy Young/Studio Y

Printed in the U.S.A.

IL 6+

with thanks to Ray Stoddard and the
Mercy High School Footlighters

No Time to Die

one

Jenny? Jenny, are you there? Please pick up the phone, Jen. I have to talk to you. Did you get my e-mail? I don't know what to do. I think I'd better leave Wisteria.

Jenny, where are you? You promised you'd visit me. Why haven't you come? I wish you'd pick up the phone.

Okay, listen, I have to get back to rehearsal. Call me. Call me soon as you can.

I retrieved my sister's message about eleven o'clock that night when I arrived home at our family's New York apartment. I called her immediately, if somewhat reluctantly. Liza was a year ahead of me, but in many ways I was the big sister, always getting her out of her messes—and she got in quite a few. Thanks to her talent for melodrama, my sister could turn a small misunderstanding in a school cafeteria into tragic opera.

Though I figured this was one more overblown event, I stayed up till two A.M., dialing her cell phone repeatedly. Early the next morning I tried again to reach her. Growing uneasy, I decided to tell Mom about the phone message. Before I could, however, the Wisteria police called. Liza had been found murdered.

Eleven months later Sid drove me up and down the tiny streets of Wisteria, Maryland. "I don't like it. I don't like it at all," he said.

"I think it's a pretty town," I replied, pretending not to understand him. "They sure have enough flowers."

"You know what I'm saying, Jenny."

Sid was my father's valet and driver. Years of shuttling Dad back and forth between our apartment and the theater, driving Liza to dance and voice lessons and me to gymnastics, had made him part of the family.

"Your parents shouldn't have let you come here, that's what I'm saying."

"Chase College has a good summer program in high school drama," I pointed out.

"You hate drama."

"A person can change, Sid," I replied—not that I had.

"You change? You're the steadiest, most normal person in your family."

I laughed. "Given my family, that's not saying much."

My father, Lee Montgomery, the third generation of an English theater family, does everything with a flair for the dramatic. He reads grocery lists and newspaper ads like Shakespearean verse. When he lifts a glass from our dishwasher to see if it's clean, he looks like Hamlet contemplating Yorick's skull. My mother, the former Tory Summers, a child and teen star who spent six miserable years in California, happily left that career and married the next one, meaning my father. But she is still an effusive theater type—warm and expressive and not bound by things like facts or reason. In many ways Liza was like Mom, a butterfly person.

I have my mother's red hair and my father's physical agility, but I must have inherited some kind of mutated theater gene: I get terrible stage fright.

"I don't think it's safe here," Sid went on with his argument.

"The murder rate is probably one tenth of one percent of New York's," I observed. "Besides, Sid, Liza's killer has moved north. New Jersey was his last hit. I bet he's waiting for you right now at the Brooklyn Bridge."

Sid grunted. I was pretty sure I didn't fool him with my easy way of talking about Liza's murderer. For a while it had helped that her death was the work of a serial killer, for the whole idea was so unreal, the death so impersonal, I could keep the event at a distance—for a while.

Sid pulled over at the corner of Shipwrights Street and Scarborough Road, as I had asked him to, a block from the college campus. Before embarking on this trip I had checked out a map of Maryland's Eastern Shore. Wisteria sat on a piece of land close to the Chesapeake Bay, bordered on one side by the Sycamore River and on the other two by large creeks, the Oyster and the

Wist. I had plotted our approach to the colonial town, choosing a route that swung around the far end of Oyster Creek, so we wouldn't have to cross the bridge. Liza had been murdered beneath it.

Sid turned off the engine and looked at me through the rearview mirror. "I've driven you too many years not to get suspicious when you want to be left off somewhere other than where you say you're going."

I smiled at him and got out. Sid met me at the back of the long black sedan and pulled out my luggage. It was going to be a haul to Drama House.

"So why aren't I taking you to the door?"

"I told you. I'm traveling incognito."

He rolled his eyes. "Like *I'm* famous and they'll know who you are when they see me dropping you off. What's the real reason, Jenny?"

"I just told you—I don't want to draw attention to myself."

In fact, my parents had agreed to let me attend under a different last name. My mother, after recovering from the shock that I wanted to do theater rather than gymnastics, had noted that the name change would reduce the pressure. My father thought that traveling incognito bore the fine touch of a Shakespearean romance.

They were less certain about my going to the town of Wisteria, to the same camp Liza had. But my father was doing a show in London, and I told them that, at seventeen, I was too old to hang out and do nothing at a hotel. Since I had never been to Wisteria, it would have fewer memories to haunt me than our New York apartment and the bedroom I had shared with Liza.

I put on my backpack and gave Sid a hug. "Have a great vacation! See you in August."

Tugging on the handle of my large, wheeled suitcase, I strode across the street in the direction of Chase campus, trying hard not to look at Sid as he got in the car and drove away. Saying goodbye to my parents at the airport had been difficult this time; leaving Sid wasn't a whole lot easier. I had learned that temporary goodbyes can turn out to be forever.

I dragged my suitcase over the bumpy brick sidewalk. Liza had been right about the humidity here. At the end of the block I fished an elastic band from my backpack and pulled my curly hair into a loose ponytail.

Straight ahead of me lay the main quadrangle of Chase College, redbrick buildings with steep slate roofs and multipaned windows. A brick wall with a lanterned gate bordered Chase Street. I passed through the gate and followed a tree-lined path to a second quad, which had been built behind the first. Its buildings were also colonial in style, though some appeared newer. I immediately recognized the Raymond M. Stoddard Performing Arts Building.

Liza had described it accurately as a theater that looked like an old town hall, with high, round-topped windows, a slate roof, and a tall clock tower rising from one corner. The length of the building ran along the quad, with the entrance to the theater at one end, facing a parking lot and college athletic fields.

I had arrived early for our four o'clock check-in at the dorms. Leaving my suitcase on the sidewalk, I climbed the steps to the theater. If Liza had been with me, she would have insisted that we go in. Something happened to Liza when she crossed the threshold of a theater—it was the place she felt most alive.

Last July was the first time my sister and I had ever been separated. After middle school she had attended the School for the Arts and I a Catholic high school, but we had still shared a bedroom, we had still shared the details of our lives. Then Liza surprised us all by choosing a summer theater camp in Maryland over a more prestigious program in the New York area, which would have been better suited to her talent and experience. She was that desperate to get away from home.

Once she got to Wisteria, however, she missed me. She e-mailed every day and begged me to come and meet her new friends, especially Michael. All she could talk about was Michael and how they were in love, and how this was love like no one else had ever known. I kept putting off my visit. I had lived so long in her shadow, I needed the time to be someone other than Liza Montgomery's sister. Then suddenly I was given all the time in the world.

For the last eleven months I had struggled to concentrate in school and gymnastics and worked hard to convince my parents that everything was fine, but my mind and heart were somewhere else. I became easily distracted. I kept losing things, which was ironic, for I was the one who had always found things for Liza.

Without Liza, life had become very quiet, and yet I knew no peace. I could not explain it to my parents—to anyone—but I felt as if Liza's spirit had remained in Wisteria, as if she were waiting for me to keep my promise to come.

I reached for the brass handle on the theater door and found the entrance unlocked. Feeling as if I were expected, I went in.

two

Inside the lobby the windows were shuttered and only the Exit signs lit. Having spent my childhood playing in the dusky wings and lobbies of half-darkened theaters, I felt right at home. I took off my backpack and walked toward the doors that led into the theater itself. They were unlocked and I slipped in quietly.

A single light was burning at the back of the stage. But even if the place had been pitch black, I would have known by its smell—a mix of mustiness, dust, and paint—that I was in an old theater, the kind with worn gilt edges and heavy velvet curtains that hung a little longer each year. I walked a third of the way down the center aisle, several rows beyond the rim of the balcony, and sat down. The seat was low-slung and lumpy.

"I'm here, Liza. I've finally come."

A sense of my sister, stronger than it had been since the day she left home, swept over me. I remembered her voice, its resonance and range when she was onstage, its merriment when she would lean close to me during a performance, whispering her critique of an actor's delivery: "I could drive a truck through that pause!"

I laughed and swallowed hard. I didn't see how I could ever stop missing Liza. Then I quickly turned around, thinking I'd heard something.

Rustling. Nothing but mice, I thought; this old building probably housed a nation of them. If someone had come through the doors, I would have felt the draft.

But I continued to listen, every sense alert. I became aware of another sound, soft as my own breathing, a murmuring of voices. They came from all sides of me—girls' voices, I thought, as the sound grew louder. No—one voice, overlapping itself, an eerie weave of phrases and tones, but only one voice. Liza's.

I held still, not daring to breathe. The sound stopped. The quiet that followed was so intense my ears throbbed, and I wasn't sure if I had heard my dead sister's voice or simply imagined it. I stood up slowly and looked around, but could see nothing but the Exit signs, the gilt edge of the balcony, and the dimly lit stage.

"Liza?"

There had always been a special connection between my sister and me. We didn't look alike, but when we were little, we tried hard to convince people we were twins. We were both left-handed and both good in languages. According to my parents, as toddlers we had our own language, the way twins sometimes do. Even when we were older, I always seemed to know what Liza was thinking. Could something like that survive death?

No, I just wanted it to; I refused to let go.

I continued down the aisle and climbed the side steps up to the proscenium stage. Its apron, the flooring that bows out beyond the curtain line, was deep. If Liza had been with me, she would have dashed onto it and begun an impromptu performance. I walked to the place that Liza claimed was the most magical in the world—front and center stage—then faced the rows of empty seats.

I'm here, Liza, I thought for a second time.

After she died, I had tried to break the habit of mentally talking to her, of thinking what I'd tell her when she got home from school. It was impossible.

I've come as I promised, Liza.

I rubbed my arms, for the air around me had suddenly grown cold. Its heaviness made me feel strange, almost weightless. My head grew light. I felt as if I could float up and out of myself. The sensation was oddly pleasant at first. Then my bones and muscles felt as if they were dissolving. I was losing myself—I could no longer sense my body. I began to panic.

The lights came up around me, cool-colored, as if the stage lights had been covered with blue gels. Words sprang into my head and the lines seemed familiar, like something I had said many times before: *O time, thou must untangle this knot, not I. It is too hard a knot for me t'untie.*

In the beat that followed I realized I had spoken the lines aloud.

"Wrong play."

I jumped at the deep male voice.

"We did that one last year."

I spun around.

"Sorry, I didn't mean to scare you."

The blue light faded into ordinary house and over-head stage lighting. A tall, lean guy with sandy-colored hair, my age or a little older, set down a carton. He must have turned on the lights when entering from behind the stage. He strode toward me, smiling, his hand extended. "Hi. I'm Brian Jones."

"I'm Jenny." I struggled to focus on the scene around me. "Jenny Baird."

Brian studied me for a long moment, and I wondered if I had sounded unsure when saying my new last name. Then he smiled again. He had one of those slow-breaking, tantalizing smiles. "Jenny Baird with the long red hair. Nice to meet you. Are you here for camp?"

"Yes. You, too?"

"I'm always here. This summer I'm stage manager." He pulled a penknife from his pocket, flicked it open, and walked back to the carton. Kneeling, he inserted the knife in the lid and ripped it open. "Want a script? Are you warming up for tomorrow?"

"Oh, no. I don't act. I'm here to do crew work."

He gave me another long and curious look, then pulled out a handful of paperback books, identical copies of *A Midsummer Night's Dream*. "I guess you don't know about Walker," he said, setting the books down in sets of five. "He's our director and insists that everyone acts."

"He can insist, but it won't do him any good," I replied. "I have stage fright. I can act if I'm in a classroom or hanging out with friends, but put me on a stage with lights shining in my face and an audience staring up at me, and something happens."

"Like what?" Brian asked, sounding amused.

"My voice gets squeaky, my palms sweat. I feel as if I'm going to throw up. Of course," I added, "none of my elementary school teachers left me on stage long enough to find out if I would."

He laughed.

"It's humiliating," I told him.

"I suppose it would be," he said, his voice gentler. "Maybe we can help you get over it."

I walked toward him. "Maybe you can explain to the director that I can't."

He gazed up at me, smiling. His deep brown eyes could shift easily between seriousness and amusement. "I'll give it a shot. But I should warn you, Walker can be stubborn about his policies and very tough on his students. He prides himself on it."

"It sounds as if you know him well." Had Brian known Liza, too? I wondered.

"I'm going to be a sophomore here at Chase," Brian replied, "and during my high school years I was a student at the camp, an actor. Did you see our production last year?"

"No. What play did you do?"

"The one you just quoted from," he reminded me. For a moment I felt caught. *"Twelfth Night."*

"Those were Viola's lines," he added.

Liza's role. Which was how I knew the lines—I'd helped her prepare for auditions.

Still, the way Brian studied me made me uncomfortable. Did he know who I was? Don't be stupid, I told myself. Liza had been lanky and dark-haired, like my father, while my mother and I looked as if we had descended from leprechauns. Liza's funeral had been private, with only our closest friends and family invited. My mother had always protected me from the media.

"It's a great play," I said. "My school put it on this year," I added, to explain how I knew the lines.

Brian fell silent as he counted the books. "So where will you be staying?" he asked, rising to his feet. "Did they mail you your room assignment?"

"Yes. Drama House."

"Lucky you!"

"I don't like the sound of that."

He laughed. "There are four houses being used for the camp," he explained. "Drama House, a sorority, and two frats. I'm the R.A., the resident assistant, for one frat. Two other kids who go to Chase will be the R.A.s for the other frat and the sorority house. But you and the girls at Drama House will have old Army Boots herself. I think last year's campers had more descriptive names for her."

Liza had, but Liza was never fond of anyone who expected her to obey rules. "Is she that awful?" I asked.

He shrugged. "I don't think so. But of course, she's my mother."

I laughed, then put my hand over my mouth, afraid to have hurt his feelings.

He reached out and pulled my hand away, grinning. "Don't hide your smile, Jenny. It's a beautiful one."

I felt my cheeks growing warm. Again I became aware of his eyes, deep brown, with soft, dusty lashes.

"If you wait while I check out a few more supplies, I'll walk you to Drama House."

"Okay."

Brian headed backstage. I walked to the edge of the apron and sat down, swinging my feet against the stage, gazing into the darkness, wondering. Brian had heard me say Liza's lines, but he hadn't mentioned the voices that I'd heard sitting in the audience. I thought of asking him about them but didn't want to sound crazy.

But it's not crazy, I told myself. It shouldn't have surprised me that being in a place where I couldn't help but think of Liza, I'd remember her lines. It was only natural that, missing her so, I would imagine her voice.

Then something caught my eye, high in the balcony, far to the right, a flicker of movement. I strained to see more, but it was too dark. I stood up quickly. A sliver of light appeared—a door at the side of the balcony opened and a dark figure passed through it. Someone had been sitting up there.

For how long? I wondered. Since the rustling I had heard when I first came in?

"Is something wrong?" Brian asked, reemerging from the wings.

"No. No, I just remembered I left my luggage at the front door."

"It'll be okay. I'll show you the back door—that's the one everybody uses—then you can go around and get it."

He led me backstage, where he turned out all but the light that had been burning before, then we headed down a flight of steps. The exit was at the bottom.

"This door is usually unlocked," Brian said. "People from the city always think it's strange the way we leave things open, but you couldn't be in a safer town."

Aside from an occasional serial killing, I thought.

We emerged into an outside stairwell that was about five steps below ground level. Across the road from the theater, facing the back of the college quadrangle, was a row of large Victorian houses. A line of cars had pulled up in front of them, baggage was deposited on sidewalks, and kids were gathering on the lawns and porches. Someone waved and called to Brian.

"Catch you later, Jenny," he said, and started toward the houses.

I headed toward the front of Stoddard to fetch my luggage. As I rounded the corner I came face to face with someone. We both pulled up short. The guy was my age, tall with black hair, wearing a black T-shirt and black jeans. He glanced at me, then looked away quickly, but I kept staring. He had the most startlingly blue eyes.

"Sorry," he said brusquely, then walked a wide route past me.

I turned and watched him stride toward the houses across the street.

I knew that every theater type has a completely black outfit in his closet, maybe two, for black is dramatic and tough and cool. But it's also the color to wear if you don't want to be seen in the dark, and this guy didn't want to be seen, not by me. I had sensed it in the way he'd glanced away. He'd acted guilty, as if I had caught him at something, like slinking out of the balcony, I thought.

Had he heard Liza's voice? Had he been responsible for it? A tape of her voice, manipulated by sound equipment and played over the theater's system could have produced what I heard.

There was just one problem with this explanation—it begged another. Why would anyone want to do that?

three

By the time I had picked up my suitcase, dragged it around the building, and crossed the street, the guy in black had disappeared among the other kids gathering at the four houses. Drama House, which had a sign on it, was the best kept of the three-story homes. Covered in pale yellow clapboard with white trim, it had a steep pyramid-shaped roof, gables protruding at different angles, and a turret at one corner.

A guy about my height and three or four times my width blocked the sidewalk up to Drama House, two stuffed backpacks and a battered suitcase resting at his feet like tired dogs. He gazed toward the porch, where a flock of girls chattered and laughed. "She's beautiful," he said.

I peeked around him, hoping he'd notice I wanted to get past, but he was lost in wonder. "Which one?" I finally asked.

He blinked, surprised. "What?"

"Which girl?"

He shoved his hands in his pockets and looked embarrassed. "I—I was talking about the house. It's a Queen Anne, the style built at the end of the 1800s. Look at the way they used the different shapes—triangular, rectangular, round, conical. Look at the texture in the roof and front gable."

He had a strong Bronx accent—the kind I associated with beer vendors at Yankee Stadium, not an admirer of nineteenth-century architecture. I stifled a giggle.

"If I was painting it, I'd use colors with more contrast," he went on. "Red, gold, green. Lime, maybe. Yes, definitely . . . lime." He swallowed the last word self-consciously. "I'm supposed to be over there," he muttered, slinging on his backpacks, then reaching for his suitcase. He started toward a peeling gray house that had a stuffed plaid sofa and purple coffee table on its front lawn. Obviously, a fraternity.

"Now, *that* house," I called after him, "could use a paint job."

He turned back and smiled for just a moment. Despite his thick dark hair, bristly eyebrows, and nearly black eyes, his round face looked almost cherubic when he smiled.

As he hurried on to the frat, I continued down the sidewalk to Drama House and up the steps of its wraparound porch. Four girls were gathered there in a tight group, talking loudly enough for three others to hear. I joined the quiet girls.

"So did you get yourself expelled?" asked a girl

whose head was wrapped in elegant African braids. Her cheekbones were high, her dark skin as smooth as satin.

"No, Shawna, I did not," another girl replied, sighing wearily.

"How come?" Shawna asked. "Did they keep giving you second chances?"

"Something like that."

Shawna laughed. "Well, how many times did you try, Keri?"

"Not as many as I'd planned. I found out who went to the school where my parents threatened to send me. It would be entertaining for a while, but it'd get old."

As she spoke, Keri combed long nails through her hair, which was cut short and dyed, a high contrast job in black and white. Dark pencil lined her pale eyes—sleepy, half-closed eyes. I knew that look: Liza had used it occasionally to let others know they had better do something if they wanted to hold her interest.

"Hey, Keri, Paul's back," said another girl.

"Is he?" The bored expression disappeared.

"Still hot for Paul," the tall, thin girl observed.

Shawna shook her head. "I just don't understand you, girlfriend."

"Keri doesn't want to be understood," said the fourth girl of the group. She had long black hair and velvet-lashed, almond eyes.

"I mean, he's good-looking," Shawna began, "but—"

"Oh, look who's headed this way," Keri said coolly.

"Boots," muttered the thin girl.

All of us quiet ones turned to see whom the others

were eyeing. I figured it was Brian's mother, a.k.a. Army Boots.

From a distance she appeared theatrical, with a wide scarf wrapped around her thick, bleached hair and a big gold chain around her waist, but as she got close, she looked more like a P.E. teacher and mother—with a strong jaw, a determined mouth, but lots of little worry lines around her eyes.

"Ladies," she greeted us, joining us on the porch. "How are you?"

"Fine, okay, good," we mumbled.

"I hope you can speak more clearly than that on stage," she said, then smiled. "I'm Dr. Margaret Rynne. You may call me Maggie."

I thought Brian had said his last name was Jones; perhaps she used her maiden name or had remarried.

"I'm the assistant director, and for the eight of you who have been assigned to Drama House"—she paused, counting to make sure we were eight—"your R.A., or housemother. We'll start promptly. Here are copies of the floor plan. Please find your name and locate your room."

I studied the diagram. Maggie's room, two bedrooms, a multi-bath, and the common room were on the first floor. Four bedrooms and another multi-bath were on the second, and two bedrooms and a bath were nestled under the roof. We were supposed to eat in the cafeteria in the Student Union, but there was a kitchen in the house's basement.

"On each door you'll find a rope necklace with your key attached," Maggie said. "Please remember to—"

"Who wants to switch rooms?" Shawna interrupted.

"No room switching," Maggie replied quickly. "Please be attentive to—"

"But I have to, Maggie," she insisted, fingering a braid. "I'll never be able to sleep in that room."

"You can sleep with me," Keri said. "I'm in the attic."

I rechecked the floor plan. So was I.

"Each girl will sleep in her own bed," Maggie said. "I would like to remind you all that this is theater camp, not a seven-week slumber party. When the lights go out at eleven, everyone is to be in bed. Our rehearsal schedule is a rigorous one and you must be in top form."

"But I can't be in top form if I have to sleep in that room," Shawna persisted. "My sister goes to college here, and she says the back room is haunted."

"Haunted how?" asked the thin girl, twisting a strand of her light-colored hair.

"There are strange sounds at night," Shawna said, "and cold drafts, and after the bed is made, it gets rumpled again, as if someone's been sleeping in it."

I glanced at Maggie, who shook her head quietly. The other girls gazed at Shawna wide-eyed.

"It's Liza Montgomery," Shawna continued.

Now I stared at her.

"That was her room last year, you know."

"You mean the girl who was murdered?" asked a newcomer. "The one axed by the serial killer?"

"Bludgeoned," Keri corrected with a dispassionate flick of her heavily lined eyes.

Inside I cringed.

"Four weeks into our camp," said the girl with the dark silky hair, "Liza went out alone in the middle of the night."

My stomach tightened. I should have anticipated this, my sister being turned into a piece of campus lore.

"She was found under the bridge, chased under there," the girl added.

In fact, the police didn't know why Liza was beneath the bridge—whether she was chased, lured, or simply happened to be walking there.

"She got it in the back of the head—with a hammer. There was blood like all over the place."

"Thank you for that detail, Lynne," Maggie said.

"Her watch was smashed," Lynne went on.

I struggled to act like the other girls, interested in a story that was making me sick.

"That's how the police knew it was the serial killer. He murders people under bridges and smashes their wristwatches, so you know what time he did it."

"What time did he do it?" asked a new girl.

"Midnight," said Lynne.

Twelve-thirty, I corrected silently, twelve-thirty while I was still trying to reach her.

"Well, I think that's enough for today's storytime," Maggie said, then turned to the four of us who were new. "Ladies, there was a horrible tragedy here last summer. It shook up all of us. But this is a very safe campus and a safe town, and if you follow the camp's curfew rules, there is no reason to be concerned. Keri, Shawna, Lynne, and Denise"—she pointed them out— "were here last year. And camp is camp, no matter how grown-up you get. Those of you who are new, don't be conned by the tales and pranks of the veterans."

"My sister wasn't making up tales," Shawna insisted. "The room is haunted."

"I'll take it."

The other girls and Maggie turned around. I thought Maggie was going to remind me that she had prohibited the switching of rooms, but perhaps she reasoned that Shawna's room was next to her own and seven weeks was a long time to live next to someone convinced she was sharing her bed with a ghost.

"Fine," she agreed. "And you are?"

"Jenny Baird. I was assigned to the third floor."

She made a neat correction on her own copy of the floor plan, then glanced at her watch. "We have a camp meeting and cookout at the college pavilion scheduled for five o'clock. I would like you all to deposit your luggage in your rooms and be ready to go in five minutes. Wear your key and lock your door when you leave."

There was general confusion as the eight of us pulled our luggage out of the heap and rushed toward the front door. "Don't dawdle in the bathroom," Maggie called after us.

"She means it," Shawna whispered. "She'll come in and pull you off the toilet."

One of the new girls looked back at Shawna, horrified.

"Just kidding," Shawna said, laughing in a loud, bright way that made *me* laugh.

The front door opened into a large, square foyer with varnished wood trim and a worn tile floor. The stairs rose against the back wall of the foyer, turned and climbed, then turned and climbed again. A hall ran from the foot of the stairway straight to the back of the house. The common room, where we could all hang out, was to the right of the foyer. Proceeding down the hall, there was a room on either side, Maggie's and Lynne's, then continuing on, my bedroom on one side and the multi-bath on the other.

I knew from Liza's e-mails that she had liked this room, and when I opened the door I remembered why. Its back wall had a deep double window with a built-in bench. I pictured Liza practicing every possible pose a heroine could adopt in the romantic window seat, but there was no time for me to "dawdle" and try it out.

I met up with Lynne in the bathroom, then we headed out to the front porch. When everyone had reported back, Maggie led us down Goose Lane, which ran past the backyard of the fraternity next door toward Oyster Creek.

"How do you like your room?" Keri asked as she strolled beside me, her short black-and-white hair ruffling in the breeze.

"It's nice."

"Yes," she said, lowering her voice, "if you like being next to Boots."

I shrugged. I hadn't come here to see how many rules I could break.

"Hey, guy alert," Denise called from behind us.

Everyone turned around but Maggie, who marched on like a mother goose assuming her goslings were right behind. Our group of eight slowed down, or perhaps the guys picked up their pace. However it happened, the two groups soon merged and we did what guys and girls always do, say things too loudly, make comments that seem terribly clever until they come out really dumb, while checking each other out. I saw the heavyset guy from the Bronx hanging toward the back. Far ahead Maggie stopped and gazed back at us, counting her flock, I guessed.

"So where's Paul? I thought Paul was supposed to be here," Shawna said with a sly look at Keri.

"He's here. Somewhere," a guy replied. "Mike and Brian are looking for him."

Mike? Liza's Michael? I wondered. Would a guy in love with a girl return to the place where she was murdered? No way . . . and yet I had come here and I loved Liza.

"Paul's probably back torching Drama House," another guy teased. "Hope you girls didn't leave anything important there."

"I still think it was unfair for everyone to blame last year's fire on Paul," Shawna replied. "There was no evidence."

"Oh, come on. He did it," Lynne said, "probably with the help of Liza."

"Probably to get Liza," a guy observed.

"No way," argued another. "Paul wouldn't have hurt her. He was totally obsessed with her."

I saw Keri bite her lip.

"That's what obsessed people do when they don't get what they want," the boy continued. "They get the person's attention one way or another."

I didn't like this conversation.

"I thought Paul was weird before Liza was murdered," Denise said, rubbing her long, thin arms, "but he was even weirder afterward, wanting all the details."

"Most people do want the details," Keri said crisply. "He's just more honest than the rest of you."

"Anyway, it's not strange for *him,*" observed another guy. "You ever seen the video games Paul plays? The more violent they are the better he likes them."

"Movies, too," someone else added. "I bet he watched slasher movies in his playpen."

Sounds like a terrific guy, I thought.

"Paul's great-looking—in a dangerous kind of way," Lynne said, picking up her dark hair and waving it around to cool herself. "But once he gets hooked on someone or something, he's scary."

"At least scary is interesting," Keri remarked, "which is more than I can say for the rest of you guys."

The boys hooted. The girls laughed. The conversation turned to other people who had attended camp last year.

Had Liza been aware of Paul's feelings? I wondered as we walked on. Did my sister realize that someone like that could turn on you? Call it a huge ego or simple naïveté, but Liza always believed that everyone liked her—"they like me deep down," she'd insist when people acted otherwise.

Goose Lane ended at the college boathouse. Beyond the cinder-block building were racks of sculls—those long, thin boats for rowing races—and a pier with floating docks attached. Oyster Creek, wide as a river, flowed peacefully between us and a distant bank of trees. To the left of the docks was the pavilion, an open wooden structure with a shingled roof and deck. Built on pilings over the edge of the creek, it seemed to float on a tide of tall, grasslike vegetation.

Two other groups of eight had caught up with us. Maggie conferred with a guy and girl whom I guessed were R.A.s, and the rest of us climbed a ramp to the pavilion. Inside it was furnished with wood tables and benches. I headed for its sun-washed deck, which provided a view of the creek. Leaning on the railing, I finally allowed myself to look to the left, past a small green park to a bridge, the bridge where Liza had been killed. I studied it for several minutes, then turned away.

"Are you all right?"

I hadn't realized Shawna was standing next to me. "Me? Yeah."

"You're pale," she said. "Even your freckles are pale."

"Too bad they don't fade all together," I joked. "Really, I'm all right. I, uh, look like this when I haven't eaten for a while."

She believed the excuse. "They're putting out munchies. You stay here, Reds. I'll get you some."

"Thanks."

I turned back to the water. When Liza came to this place the first day, when she saw the creek sparkling in the late-afternoon sun and heard the breeze rustling in the long grass, did she have any idea that her life would end here?

No. Impossible.

She had had so much ahead of her—a scholarship to study acting in London, a film role scheduled for spring. She had had beauty, brains, and incredible talent, and the world was about to get its first real glimpse of her. It was no time to die.

Besides, even if Liza had been a more ordinary girl, no teen believes death is waiting for her. Certainly, standing by the creek that sunny afternoon, I didn't.

four

Our director arrived by motorcycle. The guys thought it was cool. I think a middle-aged man with a big paunch straddling a motorcycle looks like a jack-in-the-box before it springs—all rolled up in himself. In any case, it was a dramatic entrance, especially since he rode the cycle across the park grass and partway up a pavilion ramp, stopped only by Maggie running down it, waving her arms frantically, screaming that the machine was too heavy.

Walker backed up his vehicle and climbed off. He was greeted like a hero, the guys swarming down the walkway to see the cycle, the girls lining up on the deck of the pavilion, like ladies watching from the top of a castle wall. When Walker removed his helmet, I saw that he was bald. A few reddish strands of hair had been recruited from a low part and combed over his dome; the remaining hair grew long enough to curl over his shirt collar.

"This is a merry troupe," he said, striding up the ramp.

Inside the pavilion we sat in a circle with Walker at the center. He asked us to introduce ourselves, say where we lived, and tell something about our interests.

My parents had known Walker Burke years ago in New York, but I couldn't remember meeting him, and if I had, I would have been too young for him to recognize me now. The autobiography submitted with my application was mostly true. Realizing that whoppers would make it too easy to slip up, I had changed only what was necessary to conceal my identity, like making myself the child of a magazine editor and his wife. I had showed the bio to the two people who had agreed to recommend me under the name of Jenny Baird so there would be no inconsistencies. When called on, I was brief.

Other kids went on and on. It took at least forty minutes to get all the way around the circle of introductions. At last the final person spoke, the heavyset guy who had admired the architecture of Drama House.

"Tomas Alvarez," he said, using the Spanish pronunciation of his first name.

"My set designer," Walker replied.

"I am?"

Applicants had been invited to submit a design for the set of the play; apparently his had been chosen. Tomas's face lit up like a Halloween pumpkin's.

"It needs revision, of course," Walker said, then rose to his feet. He wiped his neck, cricked it left and right, and rolled his shoulders. He seemed to be winding up for a speech.

"Now, people," he said, "let me tell you what I expect from you. The absolute best. A hundred percent and more. Nothing less than your heart, soul, and mind."

He began to pace.

"From eight-thirty A.M. to four-thirty P.M. you will be mine. I will work you hard, so hard that at dinnertime your faces will drop onto your plates. And after dinner I will expect more of you."

He took a pair of glasses from his pocket, a nice prop with which to gesture.

"That means I expect each of you to keep yourselves in top physical shape. I expect you to eat right, to sleep eight hours a night, and to avoid risky behavior. You are old enough to know what I mean by risky behavior."

We glanced at one another.

"You will have studying to do, lines to memorize, films to watch. Your life here will be utterly devoted to drama. You will eat, breathe, and sleep drama. You will feel as if the theater owns you. If you had something less than this in mind, you should transfer to one of those cushy New York moneymakers."

I wondered how many people were considering it.

"Other directors coddle their young actors. They treat their tender egos with kid gloves and teach them to think better of themselves than they should. What I am going to teach you is to act. Come hell or high water, you'll learn."

Welcome to drama boot camp, I thought.

"In the long run," Walker said, "you'll find the skills I teach you more useful than a New York attitude."

Clearly, he didn't like the Big Apple.

Walker then asked Maggie to go over the rules—procedures at mealtime, curfew, and special instructions for campers who opted to stay through the weekend. Brian arrived while she was talking. Curious about Mike, I glanced around, but the faces were too unfamiliar for me to notice if someone new had arrived. Brian was introduced to us as the stage manager and gave us the schedule for the coming week: auditions tomorrow, a read-through on Wednesday morning, and blocking beginning that afternoon.

"Everyone will audition and everyone will do crew work," Walker told us. "There are thirty-two of you. I'm casting twice the number of fairies, which gives us twenty-six roles. But everyone, including my six techs, will be involved at least in understudy work. Got it? Any questions?"

Tomas raised his hand and waited for Walker to acknowledge him. "About trying out," the boy said, "I'd rather not."

Walker gazed at him for a long moment. "Tomas, do you have a hearing problem?"

"No, sir."

"Do you have attention deficit disorder?"

"Uh, no."

"Do you have any excuse at all for not hearing what I just said?"

"No, sir."

"Are you fat?"

Kids snickered.

"Yes," Tomas said quietly.

"Obviously, but that's no excuse for not trying out."

It's no excuse for embarrassing him, either, I thought, though I had hung around enough shows to know there were directors who made an art form of bullying others. Not wanting to offer up myself as the next public victim, I decided to talk to Walker later about my problem with stage fright. I hoped Brian would keep his promise and ease the way for me.

Maggie ended the meeting, telling us to get to know one another and reminding us to stay in the area between the bridge and the school docks. The grills had arrived by truck, and burgers would be ready in about forty minutes.

I followed a group of kids down the pavilion ramp and into the small park, where there were swings and a gazebo.

"Hey, Jenny," Brian called, "wait a sec." He caught up and started walking with me. "I haven't had a chance to talk to Walker about your stage fright, but I didn't want you to worry. I'll do it before tomorrow, okay?"

"Thanks. He comes on strong."

Brian laughed. "Don't be snowed by him. Walker puts on a great act, but really, he's just a frustrated director who didn't make it in New York. Thanks to my mother—she knew him when she was a grad student at NYU—he can still live out his dream, creating magic moments of theater in the midst of cornfields. If there are empty seats at a show, we fill them with scarecrows."

"That's too bad," I said.

Brian cocked his head.

"I mean, I don't like him very much, but I feel bad for anyone who isn't where he wants to be."

"Oh, don't worry about Walker. Here he is king of drama, just as he always thought he should be."

I didn't respond.

"Maybe I'm being too harsh," Brian added quickly. "Try to understand. I've spent most of my life hanging around theater, and sometimes I get a little cynical about the people who do it."

I smiled at him. I knew how that was.

"I wish I could hang out with you, Jenny," he said, returning my smile, "but I'm staff and right now I'm head burger flipper."

He turned back toward the grills, which had been set up along the walkway between the pavilion and the park. I continued past the gazebo, where some of the campers had gathered, crossed the grass toward the creek, then followed a path along its bank. Plumed grasses six feet tall, like those that grew around the pavilion, gave way to a timber bulwark that lined the creek almost as far as the bridge.

After Liza died, my mother thought we should come to Wisteria and toss flowers in the water beneath the bridge, but my father said he couldn't bear it. So we huddled together in our New York apartment while Sid and a family friend accompanied Liza's body home. Now I had to see for myself the place where she had died.

I guess one expects the location of a life-changing event to be remarkable in some way, but as I approached the bridge, I saw that it was quite ordinary, supported by round pilings, its undergirding painted a grayish blue, its old concrete stained with iron rust and crumbling at the edges. Stepping into the bridge's shadow I studied the mud and stones by the water's edge, where they had found Liza, then quickly pulled back.

The guy in the black clothes was there. I leaned forward again, just far enough to see him. He was sitting on the bank beneath the bridge, staring out at the water, his wrists resting on his knees, his hands loose and still.

He suddenly turned in my direction. His eyes had changed mood, their brilliant blue darkened like the water in the bridge's twilight.

I waited for him to speak, then finally said, "I saw you inside the theater."

He didn't reply.

"You were in the balcony."

Still he was silent.

"You acted as if you didn't want to be seen."

The way he listened and focused on me, as if picking up something I wasn't aware of, made me uncomfortable.

"What were you doing?" I persisted.

"Tell me your name," he said softly.

"Jenny. Jenny Baird. You didn't answer my question. What were you doing?"

He stood up. He was a big guy, over six feet, with broad shoulders. When he walked toward me, I instinctively took a step back. He noticed and stopped.

"I'm Mike Wilcox."

My heart gave a little jerk. Liza's guy.

"Where are you from, Jenny Baird?"

"New York."

"City or state?"

"The city."

"You don't talk like it," he observed.

It was true. Mom and Dad's trained voices and their constant coaching of Liza and me had ironed out any trace of a New York accent.

"We traveled a lot," I told him. "My father kept getting different jobs. But Manhattan is home now."

"At camp last year we had a girl from Manhattan who had a schooled voice like yours. Her name was Liza Montgomery. Did you know her?"

I met his eyes steadily. "No. But I've heard about her. She's a hot topic among campers."

"I bet," he replied with a grimace. "In answer to your question: I was thinking about Liza."

"Were you close to her?"

"No. Just friends."

"But I thought—" I broke off.

He observed my face shrewdly. "You thought what?"

"I heard you and Liza Montgomery were in love."

Check the actor's hands, my father always told us. Mike's face was composed, but his hands tense, his fingers curled. "You're confusing me with Paul."

"No, Paul was obsessed with her—that's what they said. You were in love." That's what Liza said, I added silently.

"I think I should know better than they," he replied shortly.

"Today in the theater, did you hear"—I hesitated, remembering at the last minute that I wasn't supposed to know what Liza's voice sounded like—"voices?"

"I heard you reciting the lines from *Twelfth Night.*"

"Anything else?"

He gazed at me thoughtfully. "Well, Brian came in then."

"Before that—how long had you been there?"

"I arrived just before you began to speak."

Maybe, I thought, but I had heard a rustling noise well before that.

"Why?" he asked.

"Just curious."

We stared at each other, both of us defiant, each aware that the other person wasn't being candid.

"Well, I'm headed back to the party."

"Enjoy it," he said. "I'm going to stay here a little longer."

"To think about Liza?"

He nodded. "She was a very talented girl. And a friend," he added.

Liar, I thought, and strode away.

five

We arrived back at Drama House about eight-thirty that evening. Some of the girls got sodas from a vending machine and holed up in the common room to talk, but I was tired of being someone other than myself, always thinking about how to respond as Jenny Baird, and was glad to escape to my room.

While I unpacked, I thought about the things that the kids from last year had said about Liza. I didn't like the idea that a creepy guy was obsessed with her. And it bothered me that the guy she had fallen in love with now claimed they were no more than friends. Maybe I remembered Liza's e-mails incorrectly, I thought, then retrieved from my suitcase a folder of notes I had saved. Sitting sideways in the window seat, I pulled my feet up, and began to read.

Jen—Hi!

I finally made it here and it's great. I had no idea so many cute guys hung around a nothing-happening place. Lucky for me, there aren't many cute girls. But our curfew is unbelievable. 10 P.M.!!! And lights out at 11!!! I'm just waking up then. I've got a cool room on the first floor with a window seat (a real window seat! Where's Jane Austen?) and another big window to climb out of. I'll be in at 10:00 and out at 10:05.

Miss you. Miss you a lot. Love, L

P.S. Would you look for my silver barrette and mail it to me? It should be in my top drawer, or my jewelry box, or on the bathroom shelf, maybe the kitchen, check Sid's car. Thanx.

I continued reading through the batch of notes—her description of Stoddard Theater, her account of the funny things that had happened during auditions, and her reaction to Walker.

He's always criticizing me, Jen, me more than anybody else. I make him mad because I don't cringe like the others at his stupid remarks. I just stare at him. One of these days I'm going to give it back. He's a nobody acting like he's directing Broadway. Somebody's got to put Walker in his place. Looks like it'll have to be me.

There were frequent references to "Boots." Of course, given Liza's difficulty in following rules, she and

Maggie had had a few run-ins. Liza thought Brian was nice. I found only two mentions of Paul. She was aware of his interest in her, but seemed to consider him just another of her fans. Maybe she had seen too many weirdos in New York to be alarmed, I thought.

She didn't get along with Keri.

Talk about a snob! She finds the whole world boring, which, if you ask me, is the ultimate in snobbery. Her parents have given her so much that the only thing left to want is something she can't have—like Paul. In front of everybody she announced that she couldn't stand my jasmine perfume. Fine, I told her, stay away from me so you don't have to smell it—make us *both* happy!

I remembered correctly the romantic way Liza had described her relationship with Mike—Michael as she called him.

"It's Mike," he keeps saying, but I like the sound of Michael better—Mikes are guys who work at Kmart. He is so gorgeous—dark hair, blue eyes to die for, tall but not one of those skinny Hamlet types—a real guy. We're like so in love, but we both fake a little. I don't discourage the other guys who are interested in me because it's always good to keep each other wondering. But really, Jen, this is true love!!! You've got to come down and meet my incredible guy. Please come soon.

The descriptions of Michael and Liza's shared moments filled the rest of her e-mails. I remembered thinking when I first read them that Liza had finally figured out what counted, for the things she was talking about so romantically were small acts of kindness, little bits of gentleness, not wild kisses. Usually, Liza went for cool, star types like herself, and after she and the guy grew tired of showering each other with flattery, the fighting got ugly. Maybe Liza had finally fallen for a guy who was terrific on the inside, too.

And maybe I should have been gentler, I thought, not trying to force Mike to admit his feelings for my sister.

I read all the way through the correspondence and came to the last e-mail, the one that had been sent after lunch the day Liza died.

Jenny,
    Don't tell Mom and Dad, but I'm thinking about coming home. I know they won't want me to pull out of the production, but I think I have to. I've hurt someone very badly, and I don't know how to make it up. I had no idea—I didn't mean it—it's terrible. I need to talk to you.
    1:20—rehearsal's started. Talk later. L

Whom Liza had hurt, I never found out. I showed the note to the police, but they dismissed it as normal high-school stuff. The pattern of the serial murderer had been established, and his victims appeared to be random. They weren't looking for suspects who knew Liza and would have had some kind of personal motive.

I wondered again what had happened that day. Had Liza suddenly realized she was hurting Paul? Had something occurred between her and Mike? Maybe that's why he denied their relationship now. Or, had she let Walker have it between the eyes? My sister had a better command of language than she had realized and could sometimes be cruel in what she said.

It wasn't until I got her phone message that night that I checked my e-mail. If I had checked earlier, I might have reached her before she slipped out the window. If I had gone to Wisteria when Liza invited me, I might have helped her get out of whatever mess she was in. I could have been with her and kept her from venturing out the same night as the murderer.

Closing the folder, I carried it to the bureau and placed it in a drawer under a pile of shirts. Then I turned out the lamp by my bed and climbed back in the window seat. I listened to the sounds of the summer night and the mix of music and laughter that floated down from open windows. A moth flicked its wings against my screen. Though I wasn't tired, my eyelids felt as fluttery as a moth. There was a cool breeze and my head grew light, so light it could have floated off my shoulders. Closing my eyes, I leaned against the soft wire screen. My mind slipped into a strange, textureless darkness. Its edges glimmered with pale blue light.

Then my body jerked and I was alert, aware of the sound of my own breathing, quick and hoarse. I felt as if I had been running fast. I held my side, massaging it. I opened my mouth, trying to catch my breath silently, afraid to make the slightest noise.

It was swampy where I was—I could smell the creek and feel the ground ooze beneath my feet. A rooflike structure supported by pilings stretched over the dark area. I listened to the lap of water against the pilings, then footsteps sounded above. Fear flashed through me like light off a knife blade.

I made my way forward into the shallow water—slowly, so as not to make a ripple of sound. I heard the light thump of feet on wet ground, then mud sucking back from shoes. My pursuer was close—whether male or female, I couldn't tell—the night was cloudy and the person's face and body covered. I hid behind one of the pilings.

I heard the person walking slowly, prowling and listening, prowling and listening. I guessed that only ten feet remained between us. If I moved, the person would know immediately where I was. But if I waited any longer, I might get trapped.

I bolted. The pursuer was after me fast as a cat. I tripped and fell facedown, splashing into the muddy ebb of the creek. I scrambled to my feet and rushed forward again.

The tumble had jolted me, and I realized that my knees, though sore from falling, were dry. I had fallen out of the window seat and rushed toward a door, my bedroom door in Drama House. There was no muddy creek here. I was safe.

Still, I shook so badly I knocked into my bedside lamp trying to turn it on. I crept into bed and pulled the sheets up to my chin, shivering despite the July heat. I reached for the lamp a second time. The darkness retreated from the glow of the dim bulb, but I didn't dare look in the corners of the room, lest the shadows turn blue—blue like the lighting in the theater this afternoon, blue like the edges of the nightmare vision I'd just had.

It was only a dream, I told myself, a natural one to have after seeing the place where Liza had died. But the blue light . . . Please, not again, I thought.

When I was a child I had horrible nightmares, dreams as strange as they were frightening, about people and things I couldn't remember seeing in real life. All of the dreams had a strange blue cast. Waking up from them terrified, I would tell Liza, and she would put her arms around me, holding me tight. Sometimes she would tell me she had had the same dream. As I grew older I didn't believe her; still it had helped me not to feel alone. "Sweet dreams," Liza would always say, soothing me, tucking me back in bed, "sweet dreams only for you and me." Eventually the nightmares stopped.

Now I scrunched down under the sheet, sweating and shivering, missing Liza more than ever, and wondering why the dreams had come back.

SIX

We gathered in the seats of Stoddard Theater at eight-thirty the next morning. Walker came up the back steps, strode across the stage, then stopped, scanning us slowly, like a shopper carefully eyeing apples before reaching into the pile. Our nervous chatter died.

"Oh, don't be bashful," he said.

Maggie called roll. Next to Mike, two rows in front of me, sat a guy who answered to Paul McCrae, but all I could see of him was brown hair hanging thick and wavy down the back of his neck. Maggie handed out adhesive name tags, which we were to stick below our left shoulder. Anyone who put it on his or her right was corrected. Brian gave out the books.

"Put your names in them immediately," Maggie instructed. "Katie, no more free replacements of lost scripts."

"She doesn't forget anything," the girl named Katie hissed to Shawna.

Walker continued to study us. "Okay, people," he said, putting on his half-moon glasses. "I am assuming you are all intimately familiar with *A Midsummer Night's Dream* and are fully prepared and eager to impress me with your auditions. Let's begin."

"Excuse me, Walker."

His eyes rolled up over his glasses. "Maggie."

"I think we should review the plot."

His smile was a tiny bow. "You have my permission to think whatever you like. Meanwhile, I'm starting the auditions."

"And is that because you prefer to review the story halfway through, once it becomes obvious that everyone is confused—as we did last year, and the year before that, and the year before that?"

"I told you she doesn't forget," Katie whispered.

Walker sighed, then eyed us. "I believe in learning from my mistakes," he said, "but I keep making Maggie assistant director."

There were muffled laughs. I glanced at Maggie, but she didn't seem to care, perhaps because she knew what he would do next—exactly what she had suggested.

"As you all no doubt already know," Walker boomed, "there are four lovers in this play. The two guys, Lysander and Demetrius, are both in love with Hermia. Hermia is in love with Lysander, but Hermia's father has chosen Demetrius to be her husband. Meanwhile, we have poor Helena, Hermia's friend, who is hopelessly in love with Demetrius. Got it?"

We nodded.

"Like all good star-crossed lovers, Hermia and Lysander plan to run away. Helena thinks she can score some points with Demetrius by telling him of Hermia and Lysander's departure. So, what do we have? Hermia and Lysander running off to the forest, Demetrius running after Hermia, and Helena after Demetrius. We have four lovers wandering around the Athenian woods on Midsummer Night."

Walker strode back and forth across the stage as he spoke, gesturing with the script. He held our attention as if he were Shakespeare himself.

"Enter the fairies: Oberon the fairy king and Titania, the queen. They're married and they're quarreling. Oberon has a jealous, vengeful streak in him. He also has a very mischievous fairy working for him, Puck, and, with Puck's help, he plans to spread a magic flower ointment on his wife's eyes while she is sleeping. The first person, beast, or thing Titania sees when she awakens, she'll fall madly in love with."

A couple kids giggled, as if just now figuring out what would happen, which told me they hadn't read the play, at least not too well. Maggie knew what she was doing.

"Now, there are some interesting candidates for Titania to fall in love with that night," Walker continued. "A group whom we refer to as 'the rustics,' six bumbling guys, are rehearsing a play in the woods to present to the Duke of Athens at his wedding. The Duke's wedding frames the entire play. Puck has some fun and transforms one of the rustics so that he has an ass's head instead of a human one, and it is he whom Titania sees first when she awakens.

"As for the lovers, Oberon gives Puck instructions to use the flower ointment to work out their problem, that is, to make Demetrius fall in love with Helena, so the four are neatly paired up. Unfortunately, Puck gets the guys confused, and we end up with a wonderful reversal, with Demetrius and Lysander now in love with Helena and chasing her, while Hermia is left out in the cold. Got it?"

We all nodded again and Walker hopped down from the stage steps, surprisingly light on his feet.

"Now, Maggie, may we begin?"

"I'm waiting," she said with a smile.

Walker started by assigning the parts of the lovers, trying different combinations for the two guys and two girls. Watching Mike read, I was amazed at his skill. I had imagined that he had just enough talent, or more accurately, the good looks to earn a small high school part. I was wrong—or perhaps the part of a lover came quite naturally to him. I glanced around: I wasn't the only girl who had trouble taking her eyes off him.

"Jenny Baird."

I didn't respond; it wasn't the name for which I was used to snapping to.

"Miss Baird." Walker's voice could roll low like thunder. Shawna nudged me.

"Walker," Brian said in a quiet voice, "I spoke to you about Jenny, remember?"

Walker turned to Brian very slowly, demonstrating for all of us how an actor can make an audience wait for a line. "I remember. Get up there, Miss Baird."

I walked to the stage steps carrying my book.

"I can try out," I told Walker, "but I get terrible stage fright when it comes time for performance."

"Act Two, Scene Two, after Puck has exited," Walker replied, as if he hadn't heard a word I'd said.

Brian stared at him and shook his head.

"Helena," Walker said to me when I was on stage, "you've just come upon Lysander, who is sleeping. What you don't know is that Puck has put the magic ointment on his eyelids, and the first person Lysander sees—you, not his beloved Hermia—he will now be madly in love with. Not knowing what has happened, you think he's making fun of you. Pick it up on 'But who is here?'"

We positioned ourselves, Mike on the stage floor and me bending over him. I began:

> "But who is here? Lysander! on the ground?
> Dead or asleep? I see no blood, no wound.
> Lysander, if you live, good sir, awake."

Mike opened his eyes, then pulled himself up quickly, responding fervently: " 'And run through fire I will for thy sweet sake.' "

I blinked and drew back. The incredible blue of his eyes and the intensity with which he zeroed in on me made my heart jolt, made me feel as if I were on an elevator that had suddenly dropped from beneath me. All I could do was stare at him, surprised. Of course, the character of Helena would have reacted the same way. I wasn't acting, but I looked like I was.

" 'Transparent Helena,' " Mike began softly, kneeling now, his eyes, his whole person focused on me, the way a lover's would be. My heart did strange flip-floppy things. I struggled to make sense of the instinctive way I responded to Mike; in the play, Helena struggled to make sense of Lysander.

I dutifully told Lysander why he should be happy with his Hermia.

" 'Content with Hermia?' " Mike responded. " 'No, I do repent the tedious minutes I have with her spent.' " He reached out and touched my face. I tingled at the brush of his fingers and could feel my cheeks getting pink. Of course, Helena's cheeks would have reddened as she got increasingly angry at Lysander.

" 'Not Hermia, but Helena I love,' " Mike said. " 'Who will not change a raven for a dove?' "

But *I* was the raven and Liza his dove, I wanted to say. I stood up quickly, feeling mixed up, caught between the play world and the real one. He gazed at me as if his eyes would hold and cherish what his hands could not. I reminded myself that this was acting.

At last he got to the end of his lines, and I pulled myself together. I was mad—mad at him for using his eyes and voice that way, madder at myself for being caught in their spell. Hadn't I seen a million actors deliver lines like that? Hadn't I fallen for not one, but two guys who were pretending to like me because they wanted to know Liza?

Just as anger was boiling up in me, it was bursting from poor Helena: " 'Wherefore was I to this keen mockery born?' " I exclaimed—ironically, totally in character.

Finishing my speech, I exited quickly, exactly as Helena should have. In fact, I wanted to run back to my seat, but I figured that Walker, upon observing my flight, would make me stay and read some more. I stopped onstage about twenty feet from Mike, waiting to be dismissed by Walker.

He looked from Mike to me, then turned to Brian. "Your new best friend doesn't seem all that shy," he observed. "I believe she has some talent."

"I never said she didn't," Brian replied coolly.

"You two are done," Walker said to us. "For now."

Mike headed for the steps stage left, I went stage right.

Lynne was called on to read as Hermia. She was so strong in the role she made the guy who played opposite her look good. Shawna tried out as Helena and Queen Titania, then Keri read for the queen's role opposite Paul as Oberon.

"No accents, Keri," Walker told her halfway through. "Save that lovely Jersey British for New York, where they can't tell the difference."

Paul was destined to be Oberon, I thought. His face was handsome, a model's face, and yet there was something wasted about it. His green eyes had circles under them—right for a jealous and somewhat vengeful king of the fairies. His body was hard—wiry, like a rock star's, his hands strong and expressive, but too thin, a thinness that could suggest cruelty.

By lunch everyone had read but Tomas, the heavyset guy who had said he'd "rather not." I thought Walker was showing some heart, or perhaps knew better than to torture the guy who had provided the winning set design for the play. I was wrong.

"All right, Tomas," Walker said as soon as we had gathered again, "this is your big chance."

Tomas was jolted out of what appeared to be the beginning of an afternoon nap.

"Get up there. You're Oberon."

There was a snicker from the vets. If Tomas played any role, it would have to be one of the rustics; there was no way he was going to prance around the stage as if there were magic in his feet.

"Paul, you're Puck," Walker said.

The contrast between the two guys was striking, and I wondered if Walker was pairing them up for his own amusement.

"Kimberly, you're Hermia." A blond girl giggled and made her way to the stage.

"Mike, Demetrius again. Act Three, Scene Two," Walker said, when the cast had assembled. "Puck is reporting back to Oberon about how he fared with the magic ointment. Demetrius and Hermia enter, and it is discovered by Oberon and Puck that Puck got the wrong guy when he tried to fix things for the lovers. Got it? Take it from the top, Oberon. Oberon?"

Tomas was paging frantically through the book; the more quickly he tried to find the scene, the harder it became. Kimberly giggled annoyingly. Paul finally snatched the script and found the page. When he shoved the book back in Tomas's face, Mike walked over to the embarrassed boy, leaned close, and ran his finger down the page. "You start here," I heard him say quietly. "Then Hermia and I enter—see?—and you don't say anything more until I lie down to sleep. Okay?"

Tomas nodded. Without waiting for Mike to get back in position, he began what had to be the most painful reading I'd ever witnessed. " 'I wo-wonder if Titan be—' "

"Titania!" Walker called out. "She's a fairy, not a football team."

Kids laughed.

" '—if Titania be awak'd.' "

He didn't know how to pronounce the *k'd* and stumbled over it as if it were a piece of broken concrete. Kimberly, waiting for her entrance, rolled her eyes and made faces at her friends in the audience.

Fortunately, a long speech by Puck followed. Unfortunately, while Paul read, Tomas practiced his next few lines so intently, his lips moved and little whispery sounds came out. Paul paused halfway through his piece.

"Which one of us is talking here?" he asked, provoking more laughter.

Tomas continued to work on his lines, though silently now, with such focus that he missed his cue.

"Oberon!" Walker hollered.

Tomas looked up and promptly lost his place. When he found it again, his voice shook badly. He got through the last line before Mike and Kimberly's entrance, but he didn't look as if he were going to make it through the entire scene. As the dialogue ran back and forth between Mike and Kimberly, Tomas's face grew redder. He looked as if he was going to cry. Given his size and his bristly eyebrows, I knew it would be a terrible sight. He began blinking his eyes. He was never going to live this down.

"Excuse me." I stood up. "Excuse me."

Mike, who had just finished a line, turned with surprise, as did everyone else.

"I'd like to play Puck if you don't mind."

It was a strange request for a person with stage fright. Brian looked baffled. Maggie frowned at the interruption. But Walker studied me with a shrewd look on his face; he knew I was trying to distract people while Tomas regained his composure.

"Would you now, Miss Baird," Walker said. "That old menacing stage fright seems to be waning, does it?"

I glanced at Tomas out of the corner of my eye. "Seems to be."

"All right. Paul, sit down."

Paul stared at Walker a moment, caught off guard by the abrupt change, then slowly left the stage, pressing his lips together, giving me a smile that was meant to chill. I ignored him, glad he was walking slowly and giving Tomas time to pull himself together. Giving me time as well—I quickly bent over and stretched before climbing the steps to the stage. Onstage I worked my back, my wrists, and my ankles, knowing I looked silly to everyone in the audience and buying Tomas even more time.

"We'll start from the top," Walker said.

Of course, I thought, let's drag him through it all again. But Tomas's eyes were clear now. If I could give the scene some lightness, play with him a little, I might get him through it and he'd have a chance of surviving camp. He looked at me curiously when I placed my script next to his feet and told him not to move an inch. I withdrew to the wings and removed my sandals. Walker sat back in his seat, arms folded over his chest, waiting.

Tomas delivered his first three lines with one less stutter. I listened, measuring with my eyes the distance between him and me. When the cue came, I raced forward and sprang, executing a handspring and round-off, landing five inches from his face. He laughed.

" 'Here comes my messenger,' " he read, still laughing some. It worked well for his character. " 'How now, mad spirit?' "

I had done gymnastic routines to music, but never to Shakespeare's iambic pentameter. The report to Oberon ran twenty-nine lines. I performed only easy stunts and thoroughly mashed my script, but I kept everyone entertained—most important, Tomas. I made sure to finish up close to him so I could give him a nudge if he missed his cue, but he was ready for me. We ran through a bit of dialogue, and Mike and Kimberly entered to read their parts. Then it was our turn again with lines Tomas hadn't yet read, but he did okay, I guessed because he felt more relaxed.

When we finished, some of the kids broke into applause. Walker didn't say a word, just went on to the next group. I had probably ticked him off. I wondered what Mike was thinking. I was careful not to look at him; hoping for his approval seemed too much like competing with Liza.

The audition went on with Walker trying different combinations of actors. He dismissed us at four o'clock, a half hour early, instructing us to read the play once again for tomorrow. The cast would be posted in the morning.

Brian showed the group the way down to the back exit and we filed out quietly. As I reached the grass outside, someone yanked on me from behind, pulling my arm so hard it hurt, forcing me to turn around.

"That role was mine," Paul said.

I could have insisted that I didn't want to play Puck, but he wouldn't have believed me, and if I explained why I had interrupted the scene, I'd embarrass Tomas.

"My name is Jenny," I told him. "If you want me, call my name, okay?"

"There's only one girl I ever wanted."

I could guess who.

"Since you're new around here, Jenny, I'm going to give you some advice." He gazed at my mouth, the only feature of mine that was like Liza's. "Watch your step. Don't play too many games with people. Don't cross Walker. Last summer there was a talented actress who did, and she ended up dead."

For a moment I could say nothing. "If you mean Liza Montgomery, I believe she was the victim of a serial killer."

"That's what people say," Paul replied, walking past me. "That's what people say."

seven

Keri and Mike hurried after Paul and a stream of campers followed. Realizing that I had better straighten things out with Brian and that this would be a good time to catch him alone, I ducked back inside Stoddard. I found him walking down the ground floor hall, deep in thought, jangling a ring of keys.

"Can I talk to you?"

Brian turned around. "Sure. What's up, Jenny?"

"I want to apologize. I shouldn't have gotten you involved with my stage fright stuff."

"No problem," he assured me.

"And I want to explain about playing Puck."

Brian grinned. "I have to admit you had me very confused for a moment, then I figured you were rescuing the fat guy."

"Tomas," I said, wanting Brian to use his name.

"*Tomas.* Really, there's no need to apologize. It was

worth it to see someone stand up to Walker. Most people don't."

"Why does Walker act the way he does?" I asked. "One moment he's nice, the next moment, obnoxious and insulting."

"It's how he keeps control," Brian replied. "Walker would say it's how he gets the best from us. Since we never know what's coming next, we stay on our toes."

"Why do *you* put up with him?"

"Good question." Brian leaned against the stairway railing and smiled that slow-breaking smile of his. "Basically, for the money and experience. I can't go to L.A. broke. I can't go there with nothing on my résumé."

"You mean to do film?"

He nodded. "Of course, it annoys Walker that I'd choose film over stage. It shouldn't matter to him, since he's always telling me I can't act. But Walker has this loyalty thing. The way he sees it, everyone is either for him or against him, there's no in-between. He takes everything personally."

I could imagine how personally he took Liza's response to him. "That's a narrow way of looking at the world."

"It's a very egotistical way," Brian replied. "And stupid. I mean, in the end, everybody is out there for himself. Sometimes it makes a person seem for you. Sometimes it makes a person seem against you."

"*That's* a very cynical view!"

"Probably." He smiled at me, then continued down the hall.

I'd had enough of theater types, and when I exited the building, I turned away from Drama House, heading left on Ink Street, the road that separated the quad from the houses, then taking another left on Scarborough, walking toward the main street of town. I remembered from Liza's e-mails that there was a café called Tea Leaves with terrific pastries and cappuccino.

Wisteria had to be the most peaceful town I'd ever strolled through. You could almost hear the flowering vines climbing their trellises. Every house had a sitting porch, every shop a tinkling bell on its door. Pedestrians moved much more slowly than in New York, adding to the sense of a town not subject to time. At the end of the long street of sycamores, sun glittered off the river. I walked all the way down to the harbor, then retraced my steps back to Tea Leaves.

The café was like a great-aunt's kitchen, with painted wood furniture and a linoleum tile floor, everything scrubbed clean. I had just settled down at a table with a chocolate doughnut and a cappuccino when I saw Tomas across the room from me, sitting by the big window. He gave me a small, self-conscious wave. I smiled back at him but stayed where I was.

When I looked up again, he was gazing intently out the window. His hand was moving quickly, sketching on an open pad. For fifteen minutes he managed to ignore the decadent pastry on his plate, drawing like a person possessed. I finished my doughnut and carried my cappuccino over to his table, wondering what he was working on.

"Hi."

He looked up and flushed. "Hi."

"May I sit with you?"

"Oh, uh, sure," he stammered and tried to clear a space quickly, knocking his backpack on the floor. It landed with a heavy thud. "Oh, nooo!" His head disappeared beneath the table, there was a lot of rustling around, then he popped up again. "Sorry."

"Everything okay?"

"I hope so."

"What do you have in your pack?" I asked curiously.

"Stuff. Sketch pads. Pencils. Pens. Chalks. A camera—two of them—color film and black and white. Lenses. They're in padded cases, they're okay."

"That's an awful lot to carry around."

"I like to be ready," Tomas explained. "You never know what kinds of interesting things you're going to see."

"I guess not." I leaned closer, trying to see his sketch-pad, but he was practiced at covering his work with his arms. "May I look at what you're sketching?"

He glanced down at his drawing, then passed it over.

It was a street scene showing the buildings across from the café, an old movie theater, a Victorian-looking hotel, a restaurant, and a large brick home.

"Wow, you're really good!"

"When I sketch buildings," he agreed. "I've always been better with things than people."

"May I look at the rest of the sketches?" I asked.

He nodded. "It's a new book. There's just a couple."

Two of them were of Drama House, one of a tree and patch of brick walk, another of Stoddard Theater from the outside. I admired the way Tomas used lighting to create drama and emotion.

"You know how to give buildings and objects feeling," I said. "I guess that's what makes you a good set designer."

"I love doing art," he replied happily. "People look at what you produce, rather than at you."

I imagined that both acting and athletics were miserable activities for him.

"Thanks for earlier this afternoon," he went on. "I know why you interrupted the scene."

"It was fun," I said, taking a sip of cappuccino. "Walker is lucky to have a real artist in his troupe. I hope he figures that out."

Tomas flushed again and studied his pastry. I began to talk about New York and gradually he relaxed with me. We compared notes on schools and friends and art exhibits we had seen in the city. Finishing our snacks, we walked up and down Wisteria's streets, poking around in shops. Time slipped away and we had to rush back to the meal hall. When we carried our food trays to the table area, everyone else was already seated.

I looked around for a place to sit. Keri's black-and-blond hair made her easy to spot in a crowd. She raised her head, saw Tomas and me, then leaned close to Mike, whispering something. He glanced up, then looked away. Just then Shawna held up a fork with a napkin stuck on its end and waved it like a flag.

"Come on, Tomas," I said.

"You sure?"

"About what?" I asked, though I knew what he meant and wasn't sure.

"That I'm invited, too."

"Of course you are."

"It's all girls," he observed.

"Lucky you!"

Tomas got an earful at dinner. The girls were annoyed because Maggie had announced that those of us who lived in Drama House would read together in the common room that evening.

"She says she wants to build camaraderie," Shawna said.

"Yeah, right. She wants to make sure we do our homework," Denise observed.

Several girls had already made plans to sneak over to the frats—not that we were supposed to visit unchaperoned.

"You guys, we've got to speed-read," one of them said.

Back at Drama House we tried, but Maggie wouldn't let us. Every time we rushed, she told us to slow down, explaining why this or that line was particularly meaningful. We lost more time than we gained. Two and a half hours later, just thirty minutes before curfew, we finished.

Keri and a new girl went immediately to Lynne's room, which had a first floor window, an easier exit than the fire escape. Shawna waited for me outside Lynne's door.

"Want to go with us?" she asked.

"Not tonight, thanks."

I returned to my room, turned on the bedside lamp, and carried a sketchpad belonging to Tomas to the window seat. Sitting down, I pulled my legs up on the bench and opened the spiral-bound book. Tomas had said that most of the drawings were done in New York. On the first page I discovered the carousel in Central Park, which Liza and I had ridden about a million times. I continued to turn the pages, feeling a twinge of homesickness—a park bench and street lamp, a greengrocer's striped awning and boxes of fruit, St. Bartholomew's Church. Then I found myself in Wisteria.

All three drawings were of the bridge over Oyster Creek. I studied one, tracing with my finger the dark lines of its pilings. I began to feel light-headed. The moonlit paper turned a cool silvery blue. The image of the bridge swam before my eyes like a watery reflection.

It was happening again, the same strange experience that I'd had last night and in the theater. Frightened, I tried to pull back, tried to pull out of it. My muscles jumped, my head jerked. I felt wide awake and relieved that I could focus again. But when I looked around, I wasn't in my room.

Oyster Creek Bridge stretched above me. I heard a car drive over it, its wheels whining on the metal grating, the pitch rising, then dropping away. Silence followed, a long, ominous silence.

"Liza," I whispered, "are you there? Liza, are you making this happen? Help me—I'm scared."

The image of the bridge dissolved. I could see nothing now, nothing but darkness with an aura of blue, but

I could sense things moving around me. The air was teeming with words I couldn't discern—angry words and feelings worming in the blackness.

I felt something being fastened around my wrist. I didn't know who was doing it or why and tried to pull my hand away. My arms and legs wouldn't respond.

"Help me! Help me, please."

The words stayed locked inside me. I tried to move my lips, but I had no voice.

Then a pinpoint of light broke through the darkness. I moved toward the light, and it grew larger and radiant as the sun. But something stirred in the darkness behind me and I quickly turned back. I saw another light, a smaller, dimmer image, like the reflected light of the moon. Suddenly there was the sound of breaking glass. The moon shattered.

I blinked and looked around. I was back in my room at Drama House, and the moon was in one piece high in the sky, shining down on a mere sketch of the bridge.

I clutched the art pad till its spiral bit into my fingers. What was happening to me?

When I had the blue dreams as a child, I was always asleep, but these visions were invading my waking hours. If I was awake, they had to be daydreams, imaginings about the place where Liza had died. And yet they came unsummoned like nightmares—dreams I couldn't control.

Now, more than ever, I needed Liza here to comfort me. And yet, it was the memory of her that gave these visions their terrifying life.

eight

Fear of slipping into another nightmarish vision made it difficult for me to fall asleep that night, but once I did, I slept solidly and could not remember any dreams when I awoke Wednesday morning. I walked to the meal hall with Shawna and Lynne, who reported that last night's adventure had been pretty dull. The girls had simply stood at a window of one of the frats and talked for a while to the guys.

In the middle of her analysis of this year's selection of guys, Shawna suddenly stopped and pointed to a group of kids clustered around the back door of Stoddard. "They posted the cast. Come on!"

She and Lynne rushed down the path. Tomas, who had been standing at the back of the crowd of campers, hurried toward me, grinning.

"You did it, Jenny. You did it! Congratulations! I knew you would get the part."

"Part—what part?"

"Puck," he said.

"As understudy, you mean." Please let that be what he means, I thought.

"No, no, you're it," he announced happily. "Isn't that great?"

"Yeah, *real* great . . . if you like a fairy that looks nauseated, sweats profusely, and speaks in a squeaky voice. I have to talk to Walker."

"Jenny," Lynne called to me, "you're Puck."

"Way to go, Reds!" Shawna hollered.

"I'm Hermia," Lynne called. "Shawna is Peter Quince, the director of the rustics."

"Congrats!" I turned to Tomas. "Did you get a part?"

"Not even understudy," he said with relief. "I'm head of scenery and props. This is going to be great. Want to eat? I sure do."

"You go ahead. There's something I have to take care of. Tell Shawna and Lynne I'll catch up with you at the theater."

Tomas walked on happily and I retreated to the porch of Drama House. From there I watched the four houses empty out. When it looked as if everyone had seen the posting and gone on to breakfast, I headed back to Stoddard. At the door I stopped to check the list. Mike had gotten the role of the lover Demetrius, Paul was Oberon, the jealous king of the fairies, and Keri, his queen, Titania. I—under my new "stage name," Jenny Baird—was listed next to *Puck*. Liza would have been astonished.

When I entered the building I heard voices coming

from a distance down the hall. One of them, Walker's, bristled with irritation.

"You've always got an excuse."

"I asked for a ladder," came the quiet reply. "Asked for it last Friday. When I get it, I'll do the job."

"I want it done *now*, Arthur."

I followed the voices past a series of doors marked Women's Dressing Room, Wardrobe, and Props, and reached the corner of the building, where the hall made a right-angle turn. Rounding the bend, I came upon Walker standing in an office doorway, his hands on his hips, a scowl on his face. He was talking to a man whose streaky hair was either blond turning gray or gray turning yellowy white. His veined hands had a slight tremor. Suddenly aware of me, he glanced back nervously.

"You don't need a ladder to get to the catwalk," Walker continued. "I told you before, there are rungs on the wall."

I tried to imagine this fragile man climbing the rungs to a narrow walkway hanging thirty feet above the stage. I had seen custodians like him before: tired, emotionally worn men just trying to get to the end of each day.

"Tell your boss I want to speak with him," Walker went on. "I'm tired of the crap they're sending me for custodians. You're worse than the last guy."

The custodian took a step back. "Yes, sir, I'll tell 'im. And maybe he'll climb up those rungs," he added. "You and him together."

I fought a smile. Arthur was tougher than he looked.

He walked away, his pale blue eyes glancing at me as he passed.

"Miss Baird," Walker said, "we don't meet till eight-thirty."

"I wanted to talk to you about the casting. I can't play Puck—you know I can't and you know why."

He cocked his head. "I'm afraid I don't. You do gymnastics."

"Yes, but—"

"Don't you ever compete?"

I shifted my weight from foot to foot. "Well, yes, I'm on the school team, but—"

"Performance is performance," he said. "If you can do one, you can do the other." He turned to go back in his office. "Now, if you don't mind, I—"

"I do mind," I said, following him in. "I need you to listen."

He sat in his chair and checked notes on his desk. He didn't look too interested in listening.

"We are talking about two different things," I explained. "When I compete in gymnastics, the performance is on a gym floor, not up on a stage. I don't see a sea of strange faces looking up at me. I'm not in a spotlight—the gym is fully lit. And any butterflies I get are over as soon as I start, because I can shut everyone out."

Now he was attentive.

"I don't have to interact with other actors. I'm not supposed to respond to the audience. I seal them out and concentrate on my routine."

"Concentration is essential in theater as well,"

Walker said. "You already have tremendous energy and instinctive stage presence. I am going to teach you to transfer your ability from gymnasium to theater. You'll be doing your gymnastics as Puck, giving Puck quickness and strength, making him lighter than air. Oh, yes, you'll do well."

"Maybe in rehearsal," I argued. "But I told you—"

"You mystify me, Miss Baird," he interrupted. "I checked your application last night. Unlike my friend Tomas, you listed no specific skills in set design, costume, makeup, lighting, or sound. What on earth did you plan to do here?"

I felt caught. "I, uh, I guess I thought I could overcome my stage fright, but when I saw how good everyone was, I figured this wasn't the place to do it. I don't want to sink the production."

"But you're not going to. You're going to pull this off."

"You're taking a big risk," I warned him.

"I've always been a director who takes risks. That's why I didn't make it in New York, where bottom-line mentality rules."

It was the usual artistic gripe, but I was surprised by the bitterness in his voice.

"You will discover, Jenny, that my shows, cast with a bunch of kids and produced in the boonies, are better theater, more imaginative and compelling fare than Broadway shows in which people pay to see Lee Montgomery play himself over and over again."

"Really."

"You're not a fan of his, I hope."

I wondered if my face had given me away. "I've seen him perform," I replied, "in *Hamlet.*"

"Ah, yes, he played that role a good fifteen years longer than he should have. I began to think it was a play about a man in midlife crisis."

Tell that to the people who flocked to see him, I thought, but I couldn't defend my father aloud.

"So, Puck, we understand each other," Walker said, his eyes dropping down again to the notes in front of him.

Hardly, I mused, and left.

We spent Wednesday morning reading the play aloud as a cast. A few kids sulked about not getting the parts they wanted, but most were pretty excited. Brian worked with Tomas and two other tech directors—heads of lighting and sound—putting down colored tape on the stage, mapping the set we would soon be building. In the afternoon we began blocking the play.

My part was blocked sketchily. It was decided that I'd be given certain parameters—where I had to be, by when—and that over the next few days Maggie and I would work on the gymnastic details. She had also volunteered to help with my stage fright, teaching me relaxation exercises and pacing me through extra rehearsals in which she'd expose me to increments of stage lighting in a gradually darkened theater.

Rehearsal ran late that day and was followed quickly by dinner, then a showing of *The Tempest*. Each Wednesday evening was Movie Night during which we'd watch and discuss a film of a Shakespearean production. After the movie I hung out with Shawna and two other new girls in her cozy room beneath the eaves. Everything was fine until ten o'clock, when I returned to my room.

For the first time since early in the day I was alone and had the opportunity to think about the strange visions I'd had the last two nights. I found myself glancing around anxiously and turning on lights, not just the bedside one, but the overhead and the desk lamp as well. I didn't want any blue shadows tonight.

I pulled down the shades, then drew the curtains over them. It made the room stuffy, but I felt less vulnerable with the windows covered, as if I could seal the opening through which thoughts of Liza entered my mind. It was eerie the way the visions occurred when I sat in the window where she would have sat and stood on the stage where she would have stood.

I walked restlessly about my room, then tried to read. At ten-twenty I knocked on Maggie's door.

"Jenny. Hello," Maggie said, quickly checking me over the way my own mother would have, making sure there was no physical emergency. "Is anything wrong?"

"No, but I'm feeling kind of jumpy. May I go out for a walk? I know it's past curfew, but I'll stay close."

"Come in a moment," Maggie said, stepping aside.

I was reluctant.

"Come on."

I entered the room. It was extremely neat, her bedspread turned down just so, the curtains pulled back the exact same width at each window, all the pencils on her desk sharpened and lined up. But Maggie's pink robe was a bit ratty, the way my mother's always was, making me feel more comfortable with her. She gestured to a desk chair, then seated herself on the bed a few feet away.

"Are you worried about your role in the play?" she asked.

What could I say? No, I'm worried about my dead sister haunting me. "Sort of."

"We'll get you over the stage fright, Jenny, truly we will. Tell me, do you remember how it started?"

"How?" I repeated.

"Or maybe when," she suggested.

"I don't know—I just always had it, at least as far back as kindergarten. I was supposed to recite a nursery rhyme for graduation, 'Little Bo Peep.' We have a video of me standing silently on stage, my mortarboard crooked, the tassel hanging in my face, my eyes like those of a deer caught in headlights."

She laughed. "Oh, my!"

"Why do you ask?"

"I was looking for a clue as to why stage fright happens to you. Psychologists say that performance anxiety is often rooted in unhappy childhood experiences, such as rejection by one's parents, or perhaps physical or verbal abuse by those who are close to the child."

"I wasn't rejected or abused," I said quickly. "Nothing terrible has ever happened to me." Till last summer, I added silently.

She smoothed the bedcover with her hand. "Sometimes memories of traumatic events can be repressed, so that the individual doesn't consciously remember those events, and therefore doesn't know why she is reacting to a situation that is similar in some way."

"I don't think that's it," I said politely.

"Let me give you an example," Maggie continued. "A child is wearing a certain kind of suntan lotion. That day she watches someone drown at the beach. Years later she happens to buy the same brand of lotion. She puts it on and finds herself paralyzed with fear. She doesn't know why, but she can't go on with whatever she planned to do at that moment. The smell has triggered the feelings of the traumatic event she has long since repressed. Only by remembering the event, understanding what has triggered such an extreme response, can she overcome it."

I shifted in my chair, uncomfortable with the psychological talk. "Repressed memory isn't my problem," I told her. "But I will try the relaxation exercises you mentioned."

"And the incremental exposure."

"That, too."

She smiled agreeably. "Still need a walk?"

"Yeah."

"Stay on this block within the area of the four houses we're occupying. It's perfectly safe, but I'm an old worrywart. Check in with me in twenty minutes, all right?"

I nodded. "Thanks."

For the first few minutes I sat on the front steps of Drama House and gazed at the night sky. Across the road the tall tower on Stoddard cut a dark pattern out of the glittering sky, its clock glowing like a second moon.

I walked up and down the block, then circled Drama House, curious to see my room from the outside. Just as I reached the back of the house, I heard a noise from the fraternity next door, a grunt, then a thud, like a fall that had been muffled by grass. A guy swore softly. I peered around the lumpy trunk of an old cherry tree at the same time that Mike, standing by a window of the frat, turned to look over his shoulder. He grimaced when he saw me.

Maybe he thought I'd mind my own business and walk on, for a moment later he checked to see if I was still there and grimaced again. I wasn't moving; I wanted to know what was going on.

He threw a stone against a second-floor window and someone raised the shade. "I need your help," Mike called quietly.

He waited—I guessed for his helper to come downstairs—and looked back over his shoulder a third time.

"Still here," I said.

The light in the first-floor room went on. The shade rolled up—it was the guys' bathroom. Maybe I shouldn't be looking, I thought, but of course I did. A stubborn window screen was yanked up.

"Ready?" I heard Mike ask the guy inside, then he leaned over, grunting and pulling. I stepped to the right of the tree to get a better view and saw a heap of a person on the ground, then a head come up above a set of shoulders as Mike heaved him onto the windowsill.

"Got a good hold?" Mike asked. "On the count of three. One, two—"

In the bathroom light I saw Paul's head, then torso go over the window frame.

"Glad he's not any heavier," the guy inside said, tugging on the screen.

"Splash some cold water on his face," Mike instructed, "and let him stay in the bathroom for a while."

The shade was yanked down from the inside, and Mike turned away from the window. He seemed to be debating what to do, then strolled over to me.

"Out for a walk?" he asked.

"Yes."

"I guess you know it's past curfew."

"I have permission," I said. "What about you?"

He grinned. "I don't."

"What happened to Paul?"

"Oh, nothing too bad."

"Nothing too bad like what?" I asked.

Mike gestured toward the tree. "Want to sit down?"

Under a tree, alone with him in the moonlight? I wasn't sure.

"You climb trees, don't you?" he persisted. "You must if you're a gymnast."

The first strong limb was about four feet off the ground. I hoisted myself onto it—Mike was going to help me but thought better of it. Then I climbed up to a limb that grew in the opposite direction, about seven feet high. Mike made himself comfortable on the long lower limb. I wondered if he and Liza used to sit there together.

"Paul hangs around town and gets himself in trouble

with the locals," Mike said. "I should have let him get his head split open by the giant he took on tonight. It's the only way he'll get any sense knocked into it."

"You rescued him?"

"Are you kidding? I'm not an idiot. I grabbed him and ran like a good coward."

I smiled.

"Listen," Mike said, "you've got to keep this quiet, okay?"

"Give me a reason why."

"We need Paul for the production. But more important, Paul needs us," he added, his blue eyes intense, persuasive. "Theater is the only thing that has kept Paul in school. It's what has kept him from getting into the really bad stuff. We can't get him bounced out of here."

"He makes me very uncomfortable."

"He aims to," Mike replied. "It's just an act."

"Brian said the same thing about Walker."

Mike smiled. "Don't be fooled by Walker. At heart, he's a good guy."

I must have made a face, for Mike laughed up at me. "Yeah, I can see he's got a fan in you. But really, I don't know what I'd do without him. He found grant money for me so I could attend last year and this. He has taught me more than the books I've read or any of my other teachers. I'm really grateful to him."

"I'm glad he has helped you," I said, "but I still think he's an egotistical tyrant with a nasty streak in him."

"A lot of creative people are that way."

I prickled. I'd heard that justification one too many times. "Creativity is no excuse for obnoxious behavior."

"Are you worried about performing?" Mike asked quietly.

"That's *not* my reason for disliking him."

"I didn't think it was. I just wanted to tell you that there is nothing to be afraid of. The audience is rooting for you, Jenny. They see you on stage and want you to do well. Everyone out there wants to love you."

Speaking of ego, I thought to myself, what an assumption!

"Trust me," Mike said, his face animated, "it's a blast."

"For you, maybe."

"There's nothing like it. I've been putting on shows since I was five."

"Are you part of a theater group?"

He grinned. "No, the kid of a minister. I spent a lot of growing-up years hanging around the church next to our house in Trenton. It had a stage—the altar; a balcony—the choir loft; sort of an orchestra—the organ; even costumes—my father often wondered why his vestments were wrinkled on Sundays. I put on a lot of performances for my friends, all of them unauthorized."

I laughed out loud. Mike laughed with me, gazing up at my face. His smile, the brightness in his eyes made my heart feel incredibly light. Then I remembered Liza and looked away. I could imagine her slipping out to meet him here in the moonlight.

"Anyway, my parents aren't thrilled about my dream of being an actor. My oldest brother is doing mission work in Appalachia. The second one is studying at Union Theological. And then there's me. Since I don't seem to have a religious calling, they would like me to pursue something practical, you know, something that guarantees a good salary."

"But you have to follow your heart," I said.

"Yes . . . Yes, you do."

He waited for me to meet his eyes, but I didn't. I couldn't.

"You know, some of the guys have been talking about you, Jenny."

"They have? Saying what?"

"They're disappointed that you paired off so quickly with Tomas."

"Why should it matter to them that we're friends?"

He looked at me curiously. "You really don't know, do you?" he said. " 'Her hair gives dawn its fire, her eyes give dusk its soul.' "

He knew how to use his voice to melt a girl's heart, to make a girl want to believe. I steeled myself against the seductive words. "Excuse me?"

"It's a line of poetry describing a beautiful girl, one who doesn't seem to know it."

I dug my fingernails into the bark of the tree. "Well, there's your answer, the reason I like Tomas. He's real. He's not an actor."

"What's wrong with actors?"

"They quote poetry. A girl has to be crazy to believe one," I told him. "It's far too easy for an actor to give you a good line."

"You're quick to judge."

"No," I argued. "I've had experience with theater types. After a while they can't tell real from unreal.

They believe their own creation of themselves and can't understand why everyone else isn't convinced they're wonderful."

He jumped down from the limb, then stared up at me, his eyes sparking with anger. "It's efficient, I guess, judging an individual by a group. You don't waste any time trying to know somebody."

But I don't want to know you! I thought as I watched Mike walk away. I can't risk knowing you.

Experience had taught me not to get close to guys who fell in love with Liza. I had been burned twice and knew I couldn't compete. It didn't matter that I could no longer give a guy access to my sister; if Mike knew who I was, I'd be access to his romantic memories of her. He'd start looking for traits and signs of her in me. And I wasn't setting myself up for that kind of heartache.

nine

"How are you doing, Jenny?" Maggie asked me Thursday morning.

"Good. Ready to go."

"Glad to hear it," she said. "We're going to work at the gym later today to block your movements. Walker thought it would be good if Tomas went with us. Knowing the set and being as visual as he is, he might see some possibilities we don't."

"Sounds like fun."

"Also, I'm photocopying a set of relaxation exercises and organizing tapes for you to listen to."

"Sorry to be so much trouble," I said.

"Nonsense," Maggie replied, putting an arm around me, giving me a hug. "I love a good challenge."

"Maggie," Walker called. "I need you to get maintenance. Arthur still hasn't replaced those lights."

She winked and moved on. From across the stage, Brian smiled at me.

"I know who the camp pet is," a girl said.

I turned my head to see who had spoken, then wished I hadn't. Keri was standing next to Paul and Mike, hoping for a reaction. I ignored her and called to Shawna, who had just come in.

"Jenny didn't hear you," Paul said.

"Oh, I think she did," Keri replied. "Hey, Shawna. Don't you think Jenny is the camp pet?"

"She's the camp redhead, that's for sure," Shawna answered.

"Obviously, I'm not *Walker's* pet," I pointed out.

Keri flicked her long, dark-lined eyelids. Perhaps conflict kept her from being totally bored. "Walker gave you a hard time at first," she said, "something he does with all his favorites. Usually, he doesn't share favorites with Maggie. She likes girls who aren't sure of themselves, girls she can mother. But then, there is that little problem of yours."

"Ease up, Keri," Shawna said.

"So she's adopted you," Keri continued, "made you her project for camp. And Brian is close to sending kisses from across the stage."

I glanced at Mike, who stood silently, his face providing no hint of what he was thinking. I knew my cheeks were red.

Paul laughed. Standing close behind Keri, as if he would hug her from behind, he leaned his head over her shoulder and pressed his face against hers. I saw Keri's shoulders relax, her body rest back against him.

But the glimmer in Paul's green eyes told me he didn't feel any real affection for her; he was just yanking her chain.

"I don't like Jenny," he said, his mouth against Keri's cheek. "She's not *my* pet."

Keri turned her face toward his, letting her mouth brush his mouth.

Paul's hands cupped her shoulders and he pushed her away. "You try too hard."

Keri spun around to look at him.

"The girls who are worth it don't try," Paul told her. "They are helpless to stop a guy from wanting them."

Keri's eyes flashed. "Liza was never helpless," she spat. "Only you were."

They walked off in opposite directions. Shawna, Mike, and I stood silently for a moment.

"Walker sure is good at casting people," Shawna observed. "It won't be hard for anyone to believe they're a quarreling couple."

"I don't know why he can't let go of Liza," Mike said.

As much as I didn't like Paul, I knew how Liza could haunt a person's thoughts. "It's not easy when you love someone," I said. "A year is not enough time to get over anything."

Mike's eyes met mine.

"Unless you're *acting*, of course."

"Of course," he replied stiffly.

"Did I just miss something?" Shawna asked as Mike strode away.

"Like what?"

"Well, you can begin by explaining to me why you just defended Paul, who's being ignorant and creepy. You know, he has pictures of Liza hanging in his room, hanging all around it, that's what Andrew told me."

I wriggled my shoulders at the thought of it—a museum for the dead.

"Paul needs to get on with his life. It's not like he and Liza were the love story of the century. The guy Liza was hot for was Mike."

"So I heard."

"Not that she was alone in that," Shawna added. "How 'bout you, girlfriend?"

"How 'bout me what?"

"What do you think of Mike?"

I shrugged. "He's okay."

Shawna grinned. "This place is just full of actors."

The acting began in earnest shortly after that. Walker required that we all be attentive to the blocking that was going on whether we were in the scene or not. It was slow work as we highlighted our lines and noted Walker's directions in our books—the cues on which we were to enter, or rise, or cross over, that kind of thing.

We dragged through Act 2 with the fairies. Having doubled them in number, Walker had created more parts and a lot of confusion. But the pace picked up when Oberon and Titania—Paul and Keri—began to quarrel. I watched them from the wings, waiting for my cue. Walker folded his arms over his chest, looking very satisfied when Titania finally exited with her fairies.

I waited in the wings.

" 'Well go thy way,' " the angry Oberon said to Titania's back. " 'Thou shalt not from this grove till I torment thee for this injury.' "

I began to move.

"Wait! What are you doing, Puck?" Walker barked.

I stood still. "Entering?"

"Has Oberon summoned you yet?" Walker asked. "Has he? He's king. You don't emerge till he tells you to."

I backed up.

"I want you in at the end of 'My gentle Puck,' " Walker added in a milder voice, "and I want you to move close to him. You're conspirators. That line again," Walker said to Paul.

" 'Well go thy way. Thou shalt not from this grove till I–' "

The lights flickered.

" '–torment thee.' "

The lights blinked off. We were swallowed by darkness. Someone screamed, then muffled it.

"What the . . . ?" growled Walker. "Arthur!"

Our only light was the glow of the emergency Exit signs and the strings of tiny floor lights that marked the way to them.

"Everyone stay where you are," Maggie said. "We don't want an accident."

"Brian, find Arthur!" Walker ordered.

"Does anyone have a flashlight?" Brian asked. "Even a small one on a key chain would help."

Two girls seated in the audience volunteered theirs.

"Pass the flashlights toward the center aisle," Maggie instructed.

There was whispering and nervous laughter as Brian retrieved the flashlights, then crossed the stage to the steps that led to the ground floor hall. Suddenly the whispering stopped.

"What's that?" someone asked, her voice thin with apprehension. "What do I smell?"

"Perfume," a guy answered.

I sniffed and my skin prickled. I knew the scent.

"Smells like jasmine," said another girl.

Liza's perfume. I remembered the weeks after she'd died, packing her sweaters in a Goodwill bag, smelling the jasmine. I had felt as if she would walk into our bedroom at any moment. It was a scent that haunted.

The lights suddenly came back on.

"Nobody move," Maggie commanded. "I'm doing a head count."

The vets exchanged glances—perhaps they recognized my sister's trademark scent.

"Look at Paul," someone whispered.

His eyes were shut, his lips closed and smiling. He was inhaling deeply, as if he loved breathing in Liza's scent, as if he couldn't get enough.

I felt sick to my stomach. Turning away from him, I discovered Mike watching me.

Walker paced up and down the stage, obviously irritated.

"What was the problem?" he asked when Brian emerged from behind the stage.

"I don't know. The power came back on before I reached the electrical room."

"Did you see Arthur?"

"No, but I came right back."

"All of us are accounted for," Maggie reported to Walker.

Placing his hands on his hips, Walker eyed Paul and me, then Keri in the wings with her fairies, then the kids in the rows of seats below.

"It was a nice bit of theater," he said. "We might even incorporate it in our production, releasing a certain scent through the air duct system when Puck does his magic or Titania sweeps through. That said, I don't wish to be entertained by further improvisation. Got it?"

Kids nodded and looked suspiciously at one another.

I wanted to believe it was a piece of theater, but I couldn't shake the eerie feeling I'd had the day I arrived here, the strong sense of Liza's presence. I had thought I came out of my own need for closure; now I wondered if Liza had summoned me.

What do you want, Liza?

To find things for her, it was always to find things. Had someone at the camp heard something, seen something? If I probed, would I find clues that could solve her murder?

"Miss Baird," Walker was saying, "please join us on this planet."

No way, Liza, I answered my sister silently, *don't ask me to do it.*

I'd hunt for barrettes, socks, homework, and phone numbers, but not for serial killers.

ten

The best moments of Thursday and Friday were spent in the gym with Maggie and Tomas, the three of us working on how to make Puck "lighter than air." Tomas, seeing what I could do, was full of ideas on how to rework the set to accommodate vaults and tumbles. Maggie acted different than she did at the theater. She still worried, and still was unrelenting about getting things right, but sometimes, when we'd clown around, she'd laugh. We even "played hooky" for an hour, going to a nearby store to buy leotards for me. When Maggie heard that Tomas and I would be staying through the weekend, she invited us for dinner at her home Saturday night.

I learned from Shawna that Mike, Paul, and Keri were also staying over the weekend. I avoided the three of them as much as possible Friday and saw them only from a distance walking down High Street on Saturday.

I also avoided the window seat and the bridge and kept the lights on in my room. I slept badly Thursday and Friday night, wanting to close my eyes, but fighting sleep each time I'd feel myself slipping away. Still, I got a few hours each night with no haunting images. By the time Tomas and I were walking to Maggie's house Saturday night, I had convinced myself that the strange events of the first week were simply my initial reaction to facing the place where Liza had died. My second week here would certainly be easier.

Maggie lived in a pretty wooden house on Cannon Street, one block over from High. Its front porch was welcoming with wicker chairs and pots of pink and white flowers. Brian answered the door smiling. "Any trouble with my directions?"

"No," I said, "the only trouble was keeping Tomas moving. He has to stop and look at everything." I turned to my friend. "Next time we go somewhere, I'm leading you blindfolded."

"Okay," he replied, half-listening, more interested now in peering beyond Brian to see what was in the living room.

It was a homey room, though a little too flowery for me, with prints of cabbage-size roses on the slipcovers and curtains. Brian led us through a small dining room and into a square kitchen, where Maggie was stuffing potato skins.

"What can we do to help?" I asked.

"Just enjoy yourselves," she replied. "I've got everything under control here."

Brian placed a tall kitchen stool next to Maggie for Tomas to sit on.

I thought he'd get one for me, too, but when Maggie started talking with Tomas about the dinner she was preparing, I felt a tug on my arm. Brian winked, then pulled me toward the door. I followed him to the living room, though I felt a little rude leaving Tomas and Maggie in the kitchen. I glanced back over my shoulder.

"I never get a chance to hang out with you," Brian said. "Tomas always does."

"Yes, but I'm your mom's guest, too."

"She understands my situation. I think that may be why she invited you tonight. I'm only two years older than you, but you're a student and I'm staff, so I'm not supposed to ask you for a date."

"Otherwise you would?"

He laughed in response. "Sometimes I can't believe you, Jenny! You're as naive as Tomas. You make quite a pair."

"Guess we do."

His brown eyes swept over my face, the dusty lashes making his long gaze soft. His lips parted for a moment as if he was going to say something more, but he simply smiled. I glanced around the room for something to talk about.

"Is that you?" I asked, pointing to a photograph. "Or did Superman get a lot shorter?"

"That's me, Halloween, our first year in Wisteria."

I walked over and picked up the framed picture. "You were awfully cute!"

"Do you have to use the past tense?" he asked.

I laughed. "How old were you?"

"Six, I think." He crossed the room, stood beside me

for a moment studying the photo, then sat on the love seat next to the table of pictures, leaving space for me.

I remained standing and picked up another photo. "Your mom. How pretty!"

"That's her college picture. You can sit down and look at them, Jenny."

I did, and he pulled his arm up, resting it along the back of the love seat, conveniently close to my shoulders. I wondered what to do when I ran out of pictures. I wasn't ready to get romantic with him, but I didn't want him to think I *never* would.

"Who's this?" I asked, pointing to another photo. Maggie and Brian were sitting on a picnic blanket with a child who looked two or three years younger than Brian. There were several pictures of the child, a beautiful little girl with brown hair and blue eyes. I picked up the closest one.

"That's my sister, Melanie."

"Where is she now?" I asked, then wished I hadn't. As I gazed at her face, a strange feeling came over me. I knew she was dead.

"She died about six months after that picture was taken."

"I'm sorry. I shouldn't have asked."

"Don't worry about it," Brian said. "It was a long time ago. I was only five at the time."

I kept looking at the picture. With her dark hair and puffy party dress, Melanie reminded me of a young Liza.

"What is it?" Brian asked gently. "You look so—so sad."

"It is sad," I replied, tempted to tell him what we shared. I thought about the way Maggie watched us campers like a worried mother hen. Since Liza's death, I had caught my own mother watching me that way.

I placed the picture back on the table, and Brian reached over and picked up another. "This is my favorite photo of Melanie," he said, laying it in my lap. "This is how I remember her."

I held the picture gently. His sister was wearing little green overalls with a bunny on the front. She had a wonderful, merry smile and eyes full of mischief, as if she were keeping a delicious secret.

The image grew blurry and I felt tears in my eyes, helpless tears for Brian's family and mine. I blinked them back, but the image still wavered before me, its edges softening and shifting, another image rising up through it, like an object at the bottom of a pond that suddenly clears. The little girl was in a long, narrow box and she was scared. A soft black blanket dropped down over her. I felt horribly afraid. Then Liza stood next to me. I couldn't see her, but I knew it was she. "Don't be scared, Jenny," she said. "I'll help you."

"Jen," Brian said, "Jenny!" He pulled me close to him. "I didn't bring you over here to make you sad."

My eyes cleared; the little girl was smiling up at me again. "How did Melanie die?"

"In a fire. She became frightened and hid in a closet."

My throat tightened. "In a closet?"

"The baby-sitter couldn't find her. She died from smoke inhalation."

I swallowed hard. What in the sunny picture before

me had allowed me to see her in a long box—a closet—with a blanket of black smoke descending upon her?

"Have you ever been in a fire?" Brian asked.

"No. No, it must be very frightening."

"You feel so powerless," he said.

Powerless was how I felt now, unable to stop the images that invaded my mind. I had been careful the last two days, but as soon as I let down my guard, Liza crept back into my head.

Was there something real about these images, I wondered, something true about them?

Liza and I used to watch Mom's old films and laugh ourselves silly at one called *Teen Psychic*. There were a lot of close-ups of Mom's green eyes widening with terror as she gazed at photos of murder sites and touched things that belonged to dead people. In a singsongy voice she would describe the visions she was seeing, images that would help solve mysteries. I wished I could laugh about it now, but I was scared and desperate to believe there was nothing psychic about me and my visions.

I glanced up at Brian.

"Good move, guy," he said to himself. "A girl comes over, you get time alone, and you depress the heck out of her."

I forced a smile. "I like knowing about your family—family is what makes a person who he is. And I like seeing your house," I said, seizing the excuse to get up and walk around again. "Houses are full of clues about people."

"You know a lot more about me than I know about you," Brian pointed out.

"Well, I don't have much to tell. My family's boring."

Another picture of Melanie sat on a desk, and another on a bookcase.

It would be easy to guess that the child was dead, I reasoned, since there were no pictures of her growing older. And knowing she had died, it would be natural to imagine her in a long box—a casket, not a closet—with a symbolic black blanket drawn over her. These images had been triggered simply by my empathy with Brian as someone who lost a sister. And that, of course, was why I had thought of Liza. Liza was not sending me messages from the dead, and I was not "Teen Psychic."

I pulled a worn book off the shelf, *Handbook to Acting,* and started paging through it as if I were interested.

"How do you think it's going between you and Walker?" Brian asked.

"A lot better than I thought it would."

"He likes your feistiness," Brian said. "And it doesn't hurt that you're new to theater. I know you won't believe it, but Walker is easily threatened by people with talent and experience."

"You're right, I don't believe it."

Brian laughed and swung his feet up on the love seat, sitting sideways, watching me as I closed the book and chose another.

"To understand Walker," he said, "you've got to understand his history. When he bombed in New York, he really bombed. The last show he directed, his big chance, the one he thought would bring him fame and fortune, starred Lee Montgomery."

I turned toward Brian—a little too quickly, I realized. I knew my father had worked with Walker, but I had been too young to remember anything about the situation. "It didn't do well?" I asked aloud.

"Montgomery pulled out. He saw the ship going down and jumped fast. The show sank immediately, closing three days after he left the cast."

I turned back to the bookcase so Brian couldn't see my face. "Are you sure? Did Walker tell you this himself?"

"Walker would never tell me anything he'd consider so humiliating. My mother did, last summer, when Liza Montgomery came here. I had seen Walker go after actresses he thought were prima donnas but never with such passion as he did with Liza. Of course, Liza could defend herself. She dished it back, right in front of the other kids, and wasn't shy about reminding him that he had failed in New York, that he was just some drama teacher in the middle of nowhere."

I winced inwardly. I knew how sharp Liza's tongue could be.

"I don't think she realized what a tender point it was with him. Anyway, my mother, who knew Walker from her grad school days in New York, explained the situation to me. Don't repeat it, Jenny, I wasn't supposed to."

"I won't."

There was a clinking of silverware in the next room.

"Sounds like it's almost time to eat," Brian observed.

I returned my book to its place, and he rose from the sofa. Just before I reached the dining room door, he pulled me back. "Jenny, I realize I'm blowing my chance with you," he said softly. "I promise we'll talk about all happy things during dinner and after."

We did, and there was a lot of laughter as we discussed high school life from math class to prom dates, even Maggie chiming in with a funny account of her first date. But I felt like a person split in two, one part of me chattering away and putting on a good show, the other plagued by a growing uneasiness. What had happened between Walker and my father? What exactly had happened when Liza was here? How deep did the bitterness run?

When the evening was over, Brian insisted on escorting us back to campus, even though he was off for the weekend while other Chase students covered the dorms. It took a while for Tomas to figure out that Brian was waiting for him to go inside and leave us alone. As soon as he disappeared, Brian walked me over to the porch steps of Drama House and pulled me down next to him.

"I'm not supposed to date you, Jenny."

"That's what you said before."

He leaned forward, his elbows on his knees. "I didn't think this was going to be a problem. I mean, I'm pretty good at not letting someone become important to me. I have to be if I want to make it to L.A."

"I understand."

He laughed. "How nice of you to understand, since you're the one making it a struggle for me! It would be so easy to make you important."

"Then be careful," I told him.

"I don't think I want to be." He took my face in his hands.

"You know how important the rules are to your mother," I reminded him.

"I heard it's a rule that you have to kiss a girl when you walk her home beneath a full moon."

"The moon isn't full."

He smiled and glanced toward the tower on top of Stoddard. Its clock gleamed in the dark. "This is drama camp. The clock is shining. We'll make it a moon."

He kissed me on the lips. "Good night," he said softly, then rose and walked away whistling.

I leaned against the stair railing. Brian's kiss was nice—as nice as a handshake, I thought. How could I feel romantic when there was so much else going on in my life? I debated whether I should confide in Brian, so he would understand why I couldn't get interested. Not quite yet, I decided.

He was right, the tower clock did look like a full moon. I stood up quickly. The image I had seen Tuesday night, the shattering circle of light, flashed through my mind. Perhaps the image wasn't a moon, but a clock—a watch, for I had felt something being fastened around my wrist. I grasped my wrist as I had done then and thought of Liza's watch being smashed by the murderer.

But it was my left wrist that I grasped tonight, and the left wrist in my vision. As left-handers, Liza and I wore our watches on our right. I sat back down on the steps.

Was this detail a meaningless mistake in the way my

mind re-created the events beneath the bridge, or was it true? I tried to remember what the police report said, but I had worked so hard at blocking out the facts, I couldn't recall.

Liza didn't always wear a watch. Maybe the serial killer supplied a watch if his victim wasn't wearing one and fastened it to the wrist on which a person usually wore her watch. Maybe the watch would be a clue to the killer's identity. Was this what Liza wanted me to discover?

Of course, anyone could have fastened a watch on her, then smashed it. What if someone had done so to make it look like a crime by the serial killer? I shuddered at the idea and dismissed it, for that kind of murder suggested a more personal motive. And no one could have hated my sister enough to kill her.

eleven

Sunday morning I went to church. I sat in the back and prayed my visions would go away. I knew it was a dangerous thing to do—God has a habit of answering prayers in ways different from what we have in mind.

When I returned to Drama House, I found a note from Tomas asking if I wanted to hang out in town. I changed into a sleeveless top and shorts, slipped some money and tissues in my pockets, then went next door. Tomas emerged carrying his stuffed backpack, like a snail hauling his shell.

"Would you like to put anything in here?" he asked as he adjusted the pack on his shoulders.

"Yeah, and never see it again," I teased.

We spent an hour visiting shops on side streets, then bought two iced cappuccinos and strolled down to the river. The town harbor had a public dock, a rectangular platform extending over the water and lined with benches—a perfect place to sit and sip.

Tomas pulled out his spiral pad and began to sketch. I lay my head back on the bench and sprawled in what my mother would call "an unladylike manner," happily soaking up the late-morning sun.

"Ahoy!" I heard Tomas call out.

I grinned to myself and kept my head back.

"Ahoy!" he called again.

"Are there pirates on the horizon, Tomas?"

"No, just Mike."

I sat up.

Mike waved. He was in a small boat, maybe fifteen feet long with an outboard, painted in the maroon and gold colors of Chase College. He guided the skiff toward the dock, nosing it in, then lassoing the piling next to us.

"What's up?" he asked.

"Just hanging out," Tomas said. "How about you?"

"The same, only on water. Hi, Jenny."

"Hi." I wished his eyes weren't so much like the water and sky. The anger I had seen in them the other night had disappeared, leaving them a friendly, easy blue. Like the river, they made me feel buoyant.

He turned back to Tomas. "What are you working on?"

"Just sketches—boats, docks, houses, trees, whatever I see."

"Want to see some things from the water?" Mike invited.

"Well—" I began.

"Yes," Tomas replied quickly.

But Mike had heard me hesitate. The light in his eyes dimmed. "Maybe another time," he said. "Your sketches could be ruined if they got wet."

"They won't," Tomas assured him. "My backpack is waterproof. I'll tear out a couple sheets and use my clipboard." He rummaged through his pack, pulling out an assortment of things, then putting them back in.

"What all do you have in there?" Mike asked curiously.

"Everything but a refrigerator," I told him. "I'd like to come, too, Mike."

He smiled and I felt that buoyancy again.

Tomas strung two cameras around his neck, then grasped a clipboard and pencils in one hand and his cappuccino in the other. "Ready."

"Why don't I hold your art supplies and drink while you get in?" I suggested.

Mike, looking as if he was trying not to laugh, guided the two of us down the four-foot drop into the boat. We settled onto its plank seats, Tomas in the middle, me at the bow.

"I'm glad I didn't sign out a canoe," Mike observed as we rocked back and forth.

"Next time," I replied.

"Next time I'll let you go by yourselves," he answered, smiling, then tossed us two life jackets. "When I'm chauffeur, I make people wear these."

"How about you?" I asked, when Mike didn't put one on.

"I can swim."

"So when the boat turns over and bonks you on the head and you're unconscious, you expect me and Tomas to save you?"

"Good point," he said. "After all, I am with two such graceful boaters." He put on the orange vest, grinning at me. Then he untied the rope and pushed off from the dock.

"Can anyone sign out a boat?" Tomas asked as Mike started the motor.

"You're supposed to have experience on the water and be connected to the college somehow," Mike replied. "My grandfather was from the Eastern Shore and used to take me crabbing. He lived down in Oxford, which is where the manager of the college boathouse grew up."

We puttered out of the tiny harbor. With each boat length we put between us and the shore I felt more at ease, free from the things that had been haunting me recently. The sun was warm on my skin and the breeze cool, ribboning my hair across my eyes. I drew an elastic from my shorts pocket, leaned forward to catch my blowing hair, then pulled it through the elastic in a loopy ponytail. When I looked up, Mike was watching me.

"She's beautiful!" Tomas breathed.

Mike glanced at him, startled.

"Yes, that yacht sure is pretty," I said, nodding toward the moored sailboat that we were passing.

Mike laughed and Tomas photographed the boat.

"Cool perspective! Jen, can you believe it? There are so many cool perspectives out here."

In the next forty minutes Tomas found heaven: a house with double-decker porches overlooking the river, an old bridge across Wist Creek, an abandoned mill. "I'm going to have enough stuff to draw for the next year and a half," he said, clicking away on his camera. We motored a distance up Wist Creek then turned around and headed back to the river.

"I'd like to stay out awhile longer," Mike said. "You can stay on or I can drop you back at the town dock."

"Stay on," Tomas replied immediately. "I mean, if Jen wants to."

"Sure."

We sailed past the town harbor again, then two marinas.

"That's the commercial harbor over there," Mike said, pointing toward shore. "They have all kinds of interesting boats, Tomas. See those long ones with low sides and little houses on one end? They're like my grandfather's. They're used for crabbing."

"Can we stay here a few minutes?" Tomas asked.

"I can drop anchor."

"Great! Then I can sketch."

"Is that okay with you, Jenny? You're not nodding off on us, are you?"

I was.

"I'd hate to see you fall asleep and fall overboard," Mike said, smiling. "It would be useless this time of day. The crabs don't bite when the sun's high."

"Lucky for you, I don't, either."

Mike smirked, shut off the motor, and dropped

anchor. "Lift up your seat, Jenny, and slide the board beneath Tomas's, then you can hunker down safely."

I did and Mike tossed me two extra life vests, which I placed in the bow to cushion my back. He did the same thing on his side, then pulled his sunglasses and script from a boat bag.

With the motor off it was quiet enough to hear the light scratch of Tomas's pencil, the occasional turn of a page by Mike. I nestled down happily. The gentle rocking of the boat made me feel safe as a child in a cradle. I fell into a warm, luxurious sleep.

I don't know how long I napped, but I had slept so heavily that I couldn't open my eyes at first. I just lay there, too content to stir, and listened to their voices.

"Do you think we should wake her?" asked Tomas. "I sort of hate to. She told me she hasn't been getting much sleep."

"I'm afraid she's going to get burned," Mike replied.

"We could cover her with our shirts and let her rest a little more," Tomas suggested.

"That's an idea."

There was some movement and a bit of boat rocking, then I felt a soft cloth being laid over my legs and another one over my arms.

"Her ankles are sticking out," Tomas reported.

"I'm more worried about her face," Mike replied. "I think I have sunblock. Yeah, here it is. Put some on her face."

"On her face?"

"And her ankles."

"I can't do that."

"Why not?" Mike asked.

"I just can't."

"Tomas, it's no different from helping people put on their stage makeup."

"Then you do it."

"You're closer to her," Mike pointed out.

"So switch seats."

"Why? It's no big deal," Mike said.

"You have experience," Tomas insisted. "Switch seats."

There was more movement. "Jeez! Careful."

I'd probably get us capsized, but there was no way I was going to open my eyes, not yet. This was too interesting.

"Okay," I heard Mike mutter, close to me now. "Okay."

He dabbed a bit of lotion on my left cheek, waited a moment, then rubbed it in. He added some more, then rounded a glob over my chin. He spread the lotion across my forehead and down my nose, the way my mother used to, but more slowly. He must have remembered my right cheek and added some there, working it in gently and even more slowly than before. His hand stopped, resting on my cheek. A tip of a finger touched my mouth, lightly tracing the shape of my lips.

This was how he put on stage makeup? I opened my eyes.

"Oh, hello," he said.

"Hi."

I thought he'd draw back, but he simply pushed up his sunglasses. His face was ten inches from mine and in its own shadow, his eyes bright with reflections off the water. I couldn't stop looking at him.

"I guess you're wondering what I'm doing," he said.

"Um . . ." I tried not to look in his eyes and ended up staring at his mouth. "Sort of."

What a mouth! I thought. If *he* had fallen asleep, I would have been tempted to touch it.

Why wasn't he wearing his shirt? Because you are, stupid, I reminded myself.

I tried not to stare at his muscular shoulders and found myself gazing at the bare expanse of chest between the flaps of his life jacket. I quickly lifted my eyes to focus on his ear. Cripe, even his ear was good-looking! I didn't need this—I didn't need to notice these things about Liza's old boyfriend.

"I have some fairy ointment here," he said.

"You do?"

"Magic stuff, just like Puck's. I spread it on your eyelids."

"You did?"

"As you know, you must fall in love with the first person you see upon opening your eyes."

I stared at him, speechless.

"Oops!" He pulled back. "Wrong stuff. This is sunblock."

I sat up and managed to laugh.

"We were worried about you," Tomas said.

"Redheads shouldn't go out without their sunscreen," Mike added, then handed the tube to me. "You need it from the neck down."

"Thanks."

He changed places with Tomas, and I began spreading the stuff on my neck and arms. "How are the sketches going?" I asked. "I'd like to see them."

The truth was I'd liked to have seen anything that would distract me from Mike. Brian had held my face in his hands; he'd even kissed me. Why didn't I think *his* ears were cute?

"Tomas wants to stop by the Oyster Creek Bridge to take some photos," Mike said. "Is that okay with you, Jenny?"

Just what I needed, visiting Liza's bridge with Liza's guy—talk about a reality check!

"Why wouldn't it be?"

Tomas looked up, surprised by the snap in my voice.

"Because you have gotten so much sun," Mike answered patiently. "I thought you might be feeling it."

"I'm fine. Thanks for asking," I added lamely.

Surprisingly, I didn't feel much of anything when we anchored by the bridge or slipped beneath its shadow. We passed the pavilion, ringed by the tall, plumed grass, then turned in to the floating docks that belonged to the college and tied up silently.

"I'm going to stay down here and hose off the boat," Mike told us.

"Do you need some help?" Tomas asked.

"No, it's a one-person job."

"Well, then, thanks! It was cool," Tomas said. "I mean really, really cool."

"Glad you enjoyed it," Mike replied.

"It was nice. See you," I said quietly, anxious to escape up Goose Lane.

Did Mike have any idea how he affected me? I wasn't as good an actor as he, but I doubted he could see through my rocky performance. I probably just confused him, running hot and cold as I did. In the future I'd be more careful around him. As long as I kept my distance and he didn't learn my identity, I was safe—safe from being compared to Liza and getting my heart broken again.

twelve

Monday morning Tomas, several strong guys, and Arthur moved the gymnastic equipment I needed. The athletic department had given us permission to keep it at the theater for the next six weeks.

Tomas explained to the cast and crew the changes to the set that Walker had authorized. Walker sat back looking a bit smug, as if the rough time he'd given Tomas at the beginning of camp was responsible for bringing him out of his cocoon.

As before, there would be a waterfall—shredded Mylar lit with stage lights—cascading down the back stage wall. But now a stream would run from its base, and the bridge over the stream would have a balance beam as its downstage side. The vaulting horse, disguised as a stone wall, would be placed near the right wing, its springboard offstage. For one entrance I would appear to fly forward and upward, launched from behind the curtain, then use the "wall" and my arms to propel myself even higher into a one-and-a-half twist.

"How about adding a rope?" Walker asked. "Jenny, can you shinny up and down a rope?"

"Sure."

"Brian, I want you to check out a sports store and acquire what is needed for decent climbing rope. Arthur—"

Perhaps guessing where the rope would be hung, the custodian was slinking toward the exit.

"—we're going to hang the rope from the catwalk. Put it on your list."

"When the ladder comes," he replied, and continued on.

I had a feeling I'd be climbing the rungs to attach the rope, but I preferred that so I could make sure the rope was secure.

Walker wanted to see the blocking we had worked on for Act 2, Scene 1. I was wearing a leotard beneath my shirt and shorts and began to remove my outer clothes. Out of the corner of my eye I saw Paul watching me. Of course, guys do that at gym meets and swimming pools, but his gaze wasn't the usual curious or flirty one—more like that of a cat, still and silent, observing its prey.

Keri joined him onstage since she, too, was part of the scene. I turned my back on them.

"Show 'em your stuff, Jen," Tomas encouraged me.

I would. I wanted to do both of us proud.

The scene went better than I had hoped. Though we weren't yet expected to be off book, I had spent the rest of Sunday memorizing my lines for that scene. And, as chilling as Paul could be offstage, he did his work like a professional onstage. There was spontaneous applause at the end, which made Maggie smile. Walker frowned a bit and made a few changes that I noted in my script. I was careful not to look at Mike until I was in the audience and he onstage and in character.

Walker reviewed Friday's work on the end of Act 4, then began blocking Act 5. It came to a screeching halt at the play-within-the-play that is performed by the clownish rustics—Walker doing the screeching. Shawna was on top of things, but the other five actors couldn't get straight stage left and stage right, or anything else for that matter.

Walker erupted. "What the hell are you doing?" he shouted.

The kids on stage froze and glanced at one another.

"Don't any of you listen? Do I need to put up traffic signs? If I did, would you bother to read them?" He paced the stage. "Perhaps I should get an orange vest, white gloves, and a whistle," he suggested sarcastically. "Make a note, Brian—a vest, gloves, and whistle."

Brian glanced up and said nothing.

"Did you make a note?"

"A mental one," Brian replied calmly.

"Dumbbells!" Walker exclaimed, turning on his actors again. "You're supposed to *play* ignorant people, not *be* them. When I speak, you listen. When I say something, you do it. Is that a difficult concept for you to grasp?"

The kids onstage had drawn together like a herd of sheep.

"Following directions—is this something new to you? You speak English, don't you? Next to *you*, Shakespeare's ignorant rustics are rocket scientists!"

Well, I thought, with that kind of encouragement and confidence boosting, everyone should be nervous enough to make more mistakes. Feeling bad for the kids, I made a suggestion. My father always talked about understanding the whole pattern of a play's blocking, seeing it as a large piece of choreography. I pointed out the pattern Walker was creating so that the individual directions would become clearer to the actors. I could tell from their faces that they understood.

"I get it," Denise said.

"Yeah, that makes sense," added a guy named Tim.

Shawna gave me the thumbs-up sign.

Walker sent me a cool, thankless stare. To the rustics he said, "We'll work on this after lunch."

We all figured we'd been dismissed early and started gathering our things. Then Walker turned to me. "There are fifteen minutes remaining. Puck, fairy group, Oberon, Titania. Act Two, Scene One. Let's go."

I wondered why we were doing the scene for the second time that morning.

"Brian and Doug," Walker added, addressing one of the tech directors, "I want it run with lights."

I saw Brian's eyes narrow and I realized then what was going on.

"I think that's a bad idea, Walker," Maggie said.

"And I think you're not the director," he replied, then descended the stage steps. "I want house lights all the way down, stage lights up. Doug, who do you have working with you?"

"Samantha."

Walker nodded. "Good. Do it."

I walked up on the stage knowing it was useless for me to argue. Walker was in a bad mood, my suggestion had come unsolicited, and worse, it was a good one. Now he planned to put me in my place and erase the applause from earlier that morning.

I took off my shorts, but left on my T-shirt; it made me feel less vulnerable.

"Walker, we have already discussed the best program for Jenny," Maggie reminded him. "You agreed that incremental exposure was the remedy. There is no point in doing this."

Oh, there's a point, all right, I thought.

"Places," Walker said, ignoring Maggie. "Lights."

I stood in the right wing, watching as the lighting shifted, then measured my steps back from the springboard.

"Enter Fairies and Puck," Walker directed.

I raced forward and sprang. Flying through the air, propelling myself off the horse, tucking for my rotation—I was focused totally on the gymnastics. Then my feet touched ground and I was in a flood of light, aware of a sea of dark faces below me. Fear clutched my heart. I fought it—it was stupid, irrational, senseless—but it was as strong as ever.

" 'How now, spirits, whither wander you?' " I asked the fairies, my voice thin as thread.

Katie and another girl, who split that particular fairy part, began their speech of fifteen lines:

"Over hill, over dale,
Thorough bush, thorough brier,
Over park, over pale,
Thorough flood, thorough fire. . . ."

I tried to concentrate on what they were saying, but
my stomach felt queasy. My hands grew moist.

"We do wander everywhere,
Swifter than the moon's sphere;
And we serve the Fairy Queen,
To dew her orbs upon the green."

My heart beat fast. I took deep breaths, trying to
slow it down.

"The cowslips tall her pensioners be,
In their gold coats spots you see:
Those be rubies, fairy favors,
In those freckles live their savors."

My knees shook. I was drenched with sweat. I
needed chalk to grip the beam.

" 'Farewell, thou lob of spirits,' " the fairies concluded. " 'We'll be gone. Our Queen and all her elves
come here anon.' "

The next set of lines was mine.

" 'The King doth keep his revels here tonight,' " I
said, pulling myself up on the beam as if I'd never
mounted one before. " 'Take heed the Queen come not
within his sight.' "

I rose slowly from a crouch, my heart pounding.

" 'For Oberon is passing fell and wrath because that she as her attendant hath–' "

It was unnerving the way the others watched me, as if waiting for me to slip.

" '–A lovely boy, stolen from an Indian king.' "

I struggled to keep my focus.

" 'She never had so sweet a changeling. And jealous Oberon–' "

A wave of sickness washed over me.

" 'And jealous Oberon–' "

I clutched my stomach. My mind went blank. I couldn't even think to call "line," as actors do when they forget one. I began to teeter. I caught my balance then heard a collective catching of breath.

"For heaven's sake, Walker!" Maggie chided.

"All right. House lights."

I dismounted the beam, then grasped it like a stair rail, trying to steady myself. The lights came on. Walker climbed up the steps and stood in the middle of the stage, pivoting slowly, looking us over.

"Take lunch," he said, then strode toward the back stairs. No one moved until the sound of his footsteps disappeared.

I returned to the seats to gather my things, but Shawna already had them for me. Brian spoke to his mother, and everyone else filed out quietly. I left with Shawna on one side and Tomas on the other, avoiding everyone's eyes. When we got outside, I found that Mike had positioned himself at the top of the concrete steps.

"Jenny? Jenny, look at me."

I glanced up, miserable and ashamed, knowing I could never explain my fear to someone who, like Liza, thought being onstage was "a blast."

"It takes a certain kind of person," I told him, "to believe that everyone wants to love you. And I'm not her."

⸺

Dear Uncle Louie,

I'm here at drama camp. (Thanks again for your recommendation.) I have a question, one I'd rather ask you than my father. Our director, Walker Burke, knew Dad years ago in New York. Here at camp Walker is quick to criticize New York theater and put down Dad. (Of course, he doesn't know I'm a Montgomery.) Someone here told me that Dad was in Walker's last show—that Dad pulled out of it and the show failed. Could you tell me what happened? I'm not going to say anything to Walker—I just want to know what stands between them. Thanks.

Jen

I sent the e-mail to my godfather, then took a long shower. I was grateful to Maggie for allowing me to spend lunch alone at Drama House, and I returned to the theater feeling much better. Things seemed back to normal, except that Brian was watching me a lot.

"I'm fine," I whispered to him. "Don't stare. People will notice and I don't need any more attention than I've already gotten."

Walker had decided to spend the afternoon getting the rustics straight. Tomas was told to divide the crew work among the rest of us and proved that he was more savvy about people than he let on. He gave Keri, Paul, and two others flats to paint inside, where they could be supervised, and sent Lynne and three responsible types outside with the spray paint. Two neat, quiet girls were assigned leaf stencils. Maybe he thought Mike and I were friends after yesterday: he asked us to paint the canvas that would cover the vaulting horse.

We worked on the ground floor, underneath the theater, across the hall from the dressing rooms and wardrobe. Sawhorses, drafting tables, and workbenches were spread throughout the cavernous room. There were pegboard walls of tools, shelves of paint supplies, and large rolls of canvas and paper, along with flats and screens that looked as if they had been painted over a hundred times.

After getting the other kids started, Tomas explained the job he was giving Mike and me. He unrolled a piece of prepared canvas, ten feet by five, on which he had chalked outlines of stones to create a wall. He showed us the finished version of pieces that would cover the ends of the horse and how to use varying shades of gray and brown paint to make the stones look three-dimensional.

Mike and I poured our paint and set to work. We talked little and about nothing important, but both the small talk and the silences were comfortable between us, as they were on the boat. I enjoyed the rhythm of our work, dipping and brushing, dipping and brushing. Mike began to sing to himself, snatches of songs. I giggled when a rock song wavered into a religious hymn, then shifted back into hard rock.

The music stopped. "Is something funny?"

"No," I said, but couldn't keep from smiling.

"You're laughing at my voice."

"No, just at you," I told him. "Uh, that didn't come out right."

"No, it didn't," he agreed.

I glanced up and saw his eyes sparkling.

"It's just funny the way you sing, mixing up all your songs. My friend in kindergarten used to sing like that when he finger-painted."

"So am I your friend?"

The question caught me off guard. "Sure."

He must have heard the uncertainty in my voice. "Maybe you'd like to think about it some more."

I didn't want to think about him any more than I already was. I focused on my brush strokes. Mike was silent for a while, then started singing again. Tomas stopped by to see how we were doing.

"Looks great!" he said. "When you're finished, take it to the drying room next door. You'll see clothesline there. Hang it up securely."

About three-thirty Mike and I carried our canvas to the next room. We lined it up along a rope, each of us attaching an end with a clothespin. Standing on opposite sides of our painted wall, we continued to work our way toward the middle of the ten-foot piece, clipping it every six inches. I made slower progress, having to climb up on a stool each time to reach the high clothes-line. Mike waited for me at the center.

"Do you know how many freckles you got yester-day?" he asked when I had attached the last clothespin.

"One point six million."

He laughed.

Aware of being eye level with him, feeling self-conscious, I surveyed the painted rocks, which were on my side of the canvas. "We did a good job."

"Sometimes you look at me, Jenny, and sometimes you don't. Why?"

"You expect girls to look at you all the time?"

He smiled a lopsided smile. "No. But it's as if some-times you're afraid to meet my eyes."

"I'm not," I assured him, and stared at his neck. It was strong with a little hollow at the base of his throat.

"Higher," he said.

I gazed at his mouth.

"Higher."

But when I found the courage to look up, he was look-ing down, gazing at my lips, his lashes long and dark, almost hiding the shimmer of his eyes. His face moved slowly closer to mine. He tilted his head. If I wanted to bail out, it had to be now. I held still. Feeling the nearness of him, I waited breathlessly. His lips touched mine.

How could a touch so soft, so barely there, be so wonderful? He wasn't even holding me. It was just his mouth against mine, light as a whisper.

"Hey, you guys. What have you been working on?"

We both pulled back. Shawna entered the room.

"Walker's going to keep my group till five," she

said, "but we're taking fifteen. Let's see what you've done."

"A wall," Mike said quietly.

"This side," I mumbled, stepping down from the stool. I fought the urge to touch my hand to my lips. Had his kiss felt as incredible to Liza? What had made it that magic?

Shawna ducked under the rope.

How had my kiss felt to him?

Shawna studied the canvas, then me. "You sure did get a lot of sun this weekend, Jenny," she said, smiling. "You white people ought to be more careful."

Mike flashed a sly smile over the top of the clothesline.

Shawna caught it.

"What?" she asked. "Did I miss something?"

"I didn't say anything," Mike replied.

Shawna got a knowing look on her face. "Come on, girl," she said to me. "Take a break. I need some air."

I knew I was going to be interrogated but decided I could handle that better than one more moment alone with Mike. I did not want to fall for him—fall farther than I already had.

Shawna and I took the back exit of the building, climbed to the top of the outside stairwell, and sprawled on the grass.

"Okay, Reds, what's going on between you two?"

"You two who?" I asked.

"Don't play dumb. You and Mike."

"Nothing."

"Un-hunh."

"Really, nothing!"

"That's the fastest fading sunburn I've ever seen," she remarked.

I plucked at the grass.

"Did he kiss you?" she persisted. "Is that what you were doing when I barged in?"

"Why would you even think something like that?" I replied.

"Oh, I don't know," she said, smiling. "Maybe it's those glances you keep stealing at each other during rehearsal, or maybe the way Mike murmured, 'A wall,' as if he was still feeling your kiss on his lips." She eyed me. "Whoa! There it is again, that mysterious recurring sunburn."

I bit my lip.

"Why are you fighting this?" she asked.

Because he was Liza's boyfriend and had lied about it. Because I knew I couldn't compete. Because it was scary, the spell he cast on me, the way I felt when he was near.

"He lives in Trenton," I told Shawna. "I live in New York."

"So what's that—an hour and a half by car, less by train? Ever heard of Greyhound? Amtrak? E-mail? I think you're making excuses."

I didn't deny it.

"But I'll play along," she said. "This afternoon, at least," she added with a grin, then mercifully changed the subject.

When she returned to rehearsal I went downstairs to see what Tomas wanted me to do next. Mike must have cleaned up our paints. He and Paul were in the corner of the room, Mike measuring a board, Paul standing a foot away, running his finger up and down the length of a saw. Keri sat nearby, chipping at her fingernails, looking bored.

Brian had come downstairs and was talking with Tomas. I watched them a moment, feeling proud of Tomas, the way he was managing everything and earning people's respect.

"Hey, Jen," Tomas called, "would you bring over a hammer? There's one in the toolbox right behind you."

I nodded and knelt down to unfasten the latches of the metal box. Lifting the lid, seeing that the hammer's handle was buried beneath other tools, I reached for its head, trying to extract it. I pulled back in surprise. The steel felt ice cold. Reaching down to grasp it again, I saw the metal glimmering blue. I touched it and cold traveled up my arm, as if my veins had been injected with ice. My shoulders and neck grew numb, my head light, so light I had to close my eyes.

Then I jerked and was free of the floating feeling, but I wasn't at Stoddard anymore. I stood breathless, as if I'd been running fast. Clutching my side, I opened my mouth trying to breathe silently, afraid to make the slightest noise. I could see little in the darkness that surrounded me, but I smelled the creek and heard its black water lapping against the pilings. I knew I was in terrible danger.

Soft footsteps hurried across the structure above me. I looked up and listened, trying to judge the direction the person was heading. *My* direction, I thought, panicking, no matter what, it would be my direction.

Step by step I moved forward in the darkness, hating the feel of the swampy ooze but knowing I had to keep on. About twenty feet behind me I heard the muffled thud of feet landing on wet ground.

I hid behind a piling and listened to my pursuer walking in the mud, moving steadily closer. My heart pounded so loudly I thought the person had to hear it. If he or she discovered me now, I'd be trapped.

I bolted, splashing through the shallow water. The person was after me in a flash. I tripped and fell face-down. Tasting mud, gasping for breath, I scrambled to my feet. A distance ahead I saw a wall of grass, tall as corn, and beyond that, a lighter, open area. Bright lights shone from the tops of poles. If I could make it as far as the lights, maybe someone would see me, maybe someone would help me.

Then I felt a powerful blow from behind. Pain exploded at the base of my skull. Every nerve in my body buzzed with it—every second of agony so excruciating, I could not stay conscious. I fell headfirst into darkness.

thirteen

When I opened my eyes I was in Brian's arms. He knelt on the floor next to the toolbox, holding me, searching my face, his own face lined with worry.

"Jenny, Jenny, are you all right?"

I nodded, unable to speak. The crushing pain at the back of my skull had disappeared, but the memory of it was so intense it dulled my senses and made the present seem less real. Tomas and others working on scenery had gathered around me. Paul watched me with keen eyes. Keri stood next to him, looking as if she'd finally seen something of interest. I knew Mike was next to Keri, but I didn't allow myself to look at him, afraid he'd see how much I wished he was the one holding me.

"What happened?" Brian asked gently.

"I don't know."

"Why did you faint?"

I shook my head, unable to think of an answer that would make sense to him and the others.

"Did you get lunch, Jen?" Tomas asked. "When you went back to Drama House, did you get something to eat?"

"No. I'm sure that's it," I said, seizing upon the excuse.

Brian brushed my hair back from my cheek, his dark eyes doubtful.

"I'm okay," I told him, sitting up, pulling away from him.

He let go reluctantly. Tomas, who had been searching his pockets, leaned over and handed me a candy bar.

"Perfect," I said. "Thanks."

"Why don't I walk you back to Drama House?" Brian suggested.

"No, I'm fine and want to keep working. There's the hammer, Tomas."

He picked it up, then glanced at his watch. "Everybody, let's start cleaning up. It's going to take us a while."

I stood and followed some of the others to the corner of the room where they had been cutting out leaves. Brian, shaking his head at my stubbornness, returned to rehearsal.

For five minutes I picked up scraps of paper, then, when I thought no one was paying attention to me, I walked back to the toolbox. I sorted through it and grasped a hammer, first by the handle, then by its steel head, wrapping my fingers tightly around it. Nothing, I felt nothing, just a tool that was cool to the touch like the others in the box. It didn't turn icy cold, didn't make my head grow light; nothing glimmered blue.

I walked to the bench where Tomas had been working and laid my hand on the first hammer. Just cool, I told myself, but then the cold began to seep through the tips of my fingers. It flowed through my veins and up my arm. The bench's fluorescent fixture buzzed blue. My head grew light. I quickly thrust out my other hand, grasping the edge of the workbench to steady myself.

"You doing okay?"

I let go of the hammer. "Fine."

"Sorry," Mike said, "but I don't believe you."

"I've never been better."

"Better at what? Acting?" He waited, as if he thought I would change my answer. "So I guess there's nothing I can do to help," he concluded.

"No, but thanks."

He took a step closer, leaned down, and whispered, "Just so you know, you're supposed to swoon when I kiss you, not a half hour afterward."

"That's not why I fainted."

"Darn! And I was so sure."

"Our kiss—that was just an accident," I told him.

"An accident? You mean you were aiming for someone else's lips and ran into mine instead?"

"I—I mean the kiss didn't mean anything."

"I see."

"Sometimes things just happen," I said. "They happen and don't mean anything at all."

"Really."

Paul called out to Mike then, asking for help in lifting a flat.

"Well, hope you're feeling better," Mike said, and went to help his friend.

I took a deep breath and glanced down at the hammer. I couldn't bring myself to touch it again. My blue visions were becoming like the frightening blue dreams I'd had as a child—bizarre and yet very, very real.

The *real* "Teen Psychic," I thought. What if I were? What if the images that had seemed so strange to me as a child had been retrieved from other people's minds? Maybe Liza wasn't simply comforting me after those dreams; maybe I really did share her mind and the minds and lives of others.

If so, I must have learned how to suppress the ability. But the visions I had now felt too powerful for me to control, triggered by things that formed a physical link to Liza: the window seat where she had sat, the place on stage where she had liked to stand, pictures of her murder site, and now, the hammer. I couldn't prove it, but I knew beyond a shadow of a psychic's doubt, this hammer was the weapon that had killed my sister.

Chase Library kept short hours during the summer, so I went there directly from the theater, needing a college computer to access newspaper archives. In every account I read, the facts were the same. The murder weapon was determined to be something heavy, a metal tool with a small blunt surface. The police believed it was a hammer, but the weapon had never been found. None of the news articles noted whether it was Liza's left or right wrist that bore the smashed watch.

At first I was comforted by my vision of the watch on the wrong wrist, reasoning from that small detail that the murderer hadn't known Liza. But the truth was that anyone in a hurry to escape the crime scene could have easily overlooked such a small matter.

I knew what I needed to do—carry the hammer to the bridge tonight and see what images came to me—but I was afraid. I didn't want to feel the crushing blow. Knowing what it was, realizing that I was reliving my sister's death, I felt sickened by it long after the physical pain receded.

As I gathered my things at the library, I realized that I had left my script at the theater. It was five-thirty when I reached Stoddard, but the back door was unlocked as usual, as was the room where we had been working. I retrieved my book from a bench.

Emerging from the room, I thought I heard voices at the end of the hall, but they had a strange, echoing sound, as if the people and I were separated by a very long passage. Curious, I followed the hall, rounding the corner, passing Walker's office, then Maggie's. No one was in sight. The next three doors, all offices belonging to professors, were closed. Then I saw the last door in the hall ajar and strode toward it.

I thought I was peering into a dark closet, but when I heard the voices again, I opened the door wider and saw the outline of a metal stairway. It rose inside the small, square space, four or five steps up one wall, then met the corner and turned, rising several steps along the next wall, continuing to spire up into the darkness, a murky darkness, as if there was light at the top. The steps to the tower!

I was tempted to climb them. The platform above the clock must have been high enough to command a view of both the river and creek. But the voices above me were becoming louder and more distinct. A guy and a girl—Paul and Keri, I realized—were coming down. I didn't want to meet up with them, not when I was alone. I exited quickly and hurried along the hallway. Then curiosity won out. Were they simply enjoying a romantic moment in the tower, or were they up to something? I ducked inside the room from which I had fetched my book, extinguished the lights, and hid behind the open door.

"You're losing your edge," I heard Keri say, as she and Paul walked down the hall.

Paul laughed. "I'm not here to entertain you."

"But you do entertain me," she insisted. "That little mean thing that crawls around inside your brain fascinates me."

I pressed my head against the door, watching them through the vertical crack between the hinges.

"Did you ever think that it might be crawling around in *your* brain?" Paul asked. "You don't know who I am, Keri. You keep inventing me, trying to make me into the guy you want me to be."

"That's good," she answered sharply, "real good coming from a guy who turned a girl into a fantasy, who made her so perfect in his mind he can't give her up, not even when she's a corpse."

Paul turned away so I couldn't see his face.

"Do you know why Liza went out that night?" Keri asked.

"Why don't you tell me?" he replied. "I know you want to."

"She got a note from Mike asking her to meet him by the creek."

I felt as if someone had just punched me in the stomach.

"If you're trying to turn me against Mike—" Paul began.

"I saw the note," Keri went on. "Liza couldn't wait to show me what he had written. It was poetic. He was counting the minutes till he could meet her by the water."

"Maybe you should have shared that information with the police," Paul suggested coolly.

"I've told you before, I don't go running to teachers or police. It's us against them. I'm loyal—unless, of course, someone gives me a reason not to be."

Paul faced her.

"But I find it interesting," she went on, "that a note Liza would have saved for framing wasn't found on her body or in her room. Someone must have destroyed it before the police could get their hands on it. Was it you?" She stepped close to him. "Was it?"

"Do you want it to be?" he asked, placing his hands around Keri's neck and running his fingers lightly over her skin.

For a moment she didn't say anything. She closed her eyes as if she hoped the tease would become something more, then she pushed him away.

"I just want it over," she said, her voice low and angry. "Liza's dead. Why can't you bury her?"

She turned and stalked away. I heard the outside door swing open and closed. Paul left a moment later.

I emerged from the room, still reeling from my discovery. I had made up my mind: after curfew tonight I'd go down to the bridge. I'd find out what happened when Mike asked my sister to meet him.

At eleven-thirty I climbed out the same window Liza had and followed the lane down to Oyster Creek. I didn't have the hammer with me. After Keri and Paul had left the theater, I searched the scenery and drying rooms, and even the stage, in case someone carried the tool upstairs, but I couldn't find it. I tried the tower, too, but the door had been locked.

Now, having escaped Drama House, I rushed down Goose Lane, then turned left on Scull, which ran parallel to the water. I didn't stop walking till I reached the bridge, afraid I'd lose my nerve. As I had hoped, the waterfront was deserted. I sat down quickly on the bank of the creek, pulling my knees up to my chest, pressing my face against them.

"I'm here, Liza," I whispered.

Nothing happened. My mind felt rigid like my body, locked into a protective position. I took a deep breath, rose, and walked five feet down to the edge of the water. I lay on my back beside the water and ever so slowly let go, as I had learned to do in my relaxation exercises, allowing my shoulders, my elbows, the calves of my legs to sink down into the mud and stones. I cringed when I felt the trickle of creek at the back of my skull—it felt like blood—but I continued to work through Maggie's exercises till my body and mind relaxed.

The bridge above me was lost in darkness. I turned my head to the side and gazed at the creek, at the concrete pilings and the wavering reflections of the bridge's street lamps. The water shimmered blue. I closed my eyes and still I saw blue. I grew light-headed, so light I felt as if I were floating above myself. Suspended in the air, I looked down on a dark body and a glowing watch face. Someone in black bent over the body, drew back, then smashed the watch.

I sat up quickly and grabbed my wrist, but there was no pain, not like there had been in the hammer vision. I felt confused and frustrated. Why couldn't I see who was shattering the watch? In the chase visions my pursuer was cloaked in black and had struck from behind, so I couldn't see the face. But why couldn't I now, when the person was bent over Liza?

I had thought I was inside Liza's mind reliving the events—I knew I had felt the murderer's blow as she would have felt it. Then it occurred to me: when the watch was strapped to my sister's wrist she was already dead. People who have near-death experiences talk about the spirit leaving the body, hovering above it. That was why I hovered in this part of my vision, looking down on the body and the watch face just as Liza's spirit had.

I stood up, my skin feeling clammy and chill despite the warm night. Slowly I walked toward the gazebo, running my hands through my matted hair, brushing the gritty mud from my arms.

At the gazebo I sat on the steps to think. I wondered if this was the place by the creek where Mike had met Liza. Here or the pavilion, I thought. In the pale moonlight, the pavilion, sitting high on its pilings and surrounded by tall grass, seemed its own little romantic island.

I blinked. Tall grass, grass high as corn. I had assumed the pilings of my visions were the supports beneath the bridge, but there were pilings beneath the pavilion, too, and the creek washed through the grass and under the wooden structure just as it did under the bridge. I jumped up and ran toward the pavilion, stopping at the grass jungle encircling it. It grew thick as bamboo. I thrust my arms into it, parted the long stalks, and stepped in, then continued to push aside swordlike leaves, gradually working my way through the dense vegetation. It stopped abruptly at the edge of the pavilion floor, where sunlight would end.

The moonlight ended there, too. Step by step I moved into the darkness beneath the pavilion. The ground turned soggy under my feet. I could hear the light lap of water against the pilings and small rustlings in the surrounding grass. As I moved farther beneath the structure, the water began to pool around my ankles. Mosquitoes whined in my ears. I thought I heard something and paused for a moment to listen, resting against a piling. My head buzzed and grew light. The darkness around me glinted blue.

Behind me, twenty feet back, there was a soft thud,

a sound light as a cat landing on leaves, then quiet footsteps. The person had found me.

My heart pounded in my chest. I could hardly breathe, my throat raw, my side aching from running. I slipped behind a piling hoping to see something—if not the face, the size or gait of the person—some clue as to who it was, but I couldn't. I heard the person coming closer and closer. I debated what to do.

Instinct took over. I bolted, then felt the sudden movement, the rush from behind. I wanted to pull out of the vision. I wanted it to stop now. But I had to turn around, had to reach for the face of my pursuer, to feel the shape I couldn't see.

I tried to and tripped, falling facedown in the water. Scrambling to my feet, I was too terrified to stop now. I raced forward. A hand grasped me and clamped down hard on my shoulder, fingers biting into me. I screamed and screamed. Another hand clapped over my mouth. The person pulled me back against him so violently the breath was knocked out of me. The blue light faded. The person laughed close to my ear, his moist lips touching my cheek. Paul.

"Going somewhere?"

I struggled against him, but he held me all the tighter. "Let me go!" I shouted, "Let me go!"

"Not yet."

I kicked backward, striking him in the shin.

"Don't make me get rough," he said.

"Let go, Paul. *Now!*"

"Not till you tell me what you were doing."

I continued to struggle.

"Tell me!" Paul jerked me around, lifting my whole body, making it clear who was in control.

"I was taking a walk."

"In a swamp?" he replied. "I don't think so."

I stopped struggling, deciding to save my energy for the instant he relaxed.

"I was walking through the park," Paul said, "and saw you duck under here. What a surprise"—his voice mocked me—"our best little camper, sneaking around after curfew! It's not like you, Jenny, being out late like this—it's not like the dear little Jenny we all know and love."

I didn't respond.

"Come on, talk! Are you making a pickup? Did someone leave something down here for you?"

"Nothing much," I said. "And I couldn't find it anyway."

He looked around, loosening his grip. I seized the chance to pull away from him, racing forward, then glimpsing lights through the grass, lights on poles as they were in an earlier vision—dock lights. I crashed through the grass and into a clear area, running toward the college boathouse. From a distance behind me I heard his laughter. Paul wasn't bothering with the chase. Still, I didn't stop until I reached the racks of sculls. Crouching in the shadows, I gazed back toward the pavilion.

Paul emerged from the grass surrounding it and walked toward the street. I didn't know whether he was leaving me alone or setting a trap. He knew the route I'd take back. But if he had wanted to hurt me, he would have done things differently, I reasoned; he would have kept himself hidden so I couldn't accuse him later. And if he had wanted to kill me, he would have done it under the pavilion. I could have lain there for days before anyone found me.

It was an ideal place to murder and dump a body. And I was sure from my visions that my sister had been struck down beneath the pavilion. But that wasn't where the serial murderer liked to do his killing. If the police had discovered her body beneath the pavilion, they would have searched for a different killer, someone from the town or campus. And if they had known about the hammer I found in the theater, they would have focused on the people connected to the camp. I could no longer deny the probability that Liza's killer had known her.

If that person wanted the police to think the serial killer was responsible, then Liza's body had to be transported to the bridge without leaving a trail. Given that her death was bloody, the job seemed more than one person could handle. If so, there could be two people in Wisteria who knew the truth about Liza's death.

I intended to find them.

fourteen

So what do you think, Jen?" Tomas asked me the next morning as we waited for rehearsal to begin. "You don't like it," he guessed, fingering a bolt of filmy blue fabric.

"Tell me again. I wasn't quite listening."

He patiently explained a second time how he was going to create a sky for the set by stretching his semi-transparent fabric between the thirty-foot-high catwalk that ran across the front of the stage and the eighteen-foot ridge and waterfall that formed the set's back wall.

I struggled to follow what he was saying, uneasily aware of Mike and Paul standing nearby, as if they were waiting to speak to me. I wondered if Paul had told Mike about last night's incident. It annoyed me that I had let Paul see how afraid I was, though I would have been an idiot not to have feared him in that situation.

"So what do you think?" Tomas asked again.

I glanced down at the fabric. "It's beautiful. When

the lights shine through, it will shimmer like a summer sky. "

Tomas beamed.

"Just one question. Who's attaching it to the catwalk—besides me?"

"Arthur's getting an extension ladder," he said. "Someone will volunteer. I don't think I'd better—you saw me on the boat."

Mike stepped forward. "I'll help."

"Terrific," Tomas replied. "I'll see if I can find one more person."

He headed off quickly, perhaps wanting to sidestep an offer from Paul.

Gazing upward, Paul surveyed the the length of the high, metal walkway. His face warped into a smile, as if something amusing had occurred to him. Then he turned to me. "Need some coffee this morning, Jenny?"

"No."

"You look tired," Mike observed.

Paul grinned. "That's the price of climbing out your window after eleven P.M. Yes," he added, noting Mike's surprise, "our own little Jenny."

"Why did you go out that late?" Mike's tone was disapproving.

"Someone sent me a note," I replied, "asking me to meet him by the river."

The light in Mike's eyes darkened. The muscles in his jaw tensed, hardening his face. I gave up the scrap of hope to which I had been clinging—he knew what I was referring to. He had sent the note to Liza.

"You ought to be more careful," he said.

"Yeah, you never know who you're going to meet out there," Paul added.

From across the stage Maggie called out, "Jenny. May I see you a moment?"

"She's on to you, girl," Paul whispered.

I ignored him and crossed the stage.

"How are you doing today?" Maggie asked, resting a hand on my shoulder.

"Good. Ready to go."

"Then what do you think of rehearsing with the stage lights up twenty-five percent and the house lights down about the same? Think you can handle it?"

"I'd like to try."

"I want everyone who is not in your scene to be sitting in the audience. Is that pushing you too hard? We can cut the scene immediately if you start to feel ill."

"Let's cut the scene only if I give you a signal," I proposed. "I might turn a little green, but I want to try to get through it."

Maggie smiled. "I knew from the start you'd be a great kid to work with. I'll tell Walker."

Walker wanted to run the same scene as yesterday since he thought it best to "get back on the horse you were riding when you fell off." The lights were adjusted and kids settled into their seats in the audience. Paul and Keri, as Oberon and Titania, stood in opposite wings, waiting for their entrances. Katie and her fellow fairy entered from stage left, I from stage right, vaulting, spinning, landing lightly on my feet. " 'How now, spirits, whither wander you?' "

My voice came out strong—not with as much expression as I'd have liked, but I was in control. The fairies gave their speech about how they served Queen Titania and I began my account of Oberon and his feud with the queen—the speech that I had blown yesterday.

As I spoke my lines and worked on the balance beam, I became increasingly sensitive to the stage lights in my eyes. It was like watching a sunrise and suddenly having to look away from the brightness. I paused, took a deep breath, then continued on, " 'And jealous Oberon . . . And jealous Oberon' . . . Line."

" 'Would have the child,' " Brian said softly.

" 'Would have the child, Knight of his train to trace the forest wild.' " I knew where I was again and carried on, a little shaky, but determined.

The fairies spoke the next ten lines, leading up to my favorite speech, in which Puck tells of all the mischievous tricks he likes to play. We had woven lots of gymnastics into those lines. My first stunt was a cartwheel on the balance beam.

" 'Thou speakest aright,' " I began, " 'I am that merry wanderer of the—' "

My right hand had just touched the beam. The stage lights flickered. A beat later my left hand touched. The lights went out. Total darkness. My left leg came around to find the beam but missed it. I slid off, banging my arm against the wood.

"Arthur!" Walker shouted.

"Jenny, are you okay?" It was Brian's voice.

"Fine. Fine." I was angry, not hurt. I should have been

able to complete the wheel in darkness. It was a loss of concentration, my own fault.

"Be still. Everyone be still till we get the lights on," Maggie said.

"Arthur!" Walker hollered again. "Brian, get him."

Kids giggled.

"This is nothing to laugh about," Maggie said sternly. "These pranks are dangerous. Someone could get hurt."

The nervous laughter was stifled. Kids whispered. I heard Brian's footsteps crossing the stage.

"If I find out who is behind this . . ." Walker's voice resonated in the darkness, deep and threatening. The whispers ceased.

In that moment of silence something dropped. It sounded small but heavy, like a metal object. It rolled across the stage and stopped close to me. Kneeling, I groped with my hand along the edge of the gym mat and found it. A ring.

The lights blinked on and I inspected the piece of jewelry. It was large with a gaudy red stone, the kind of ring that would be used as a stage prop. I slipped it on my finger. Glancing up, I noticed that everyone was looking at me. Katie, Keri, and Paul . . . Shawna and Lynne . . . Denise and Mike—everyone who had attended last year's camp was staring at the ring with troubled expressions. I pulled it off.

"It's from *Twelfth Night,*" Shawna said. "Remember? It's the ring Viola received, the one that Liza wore. We couldn't find it after Liza died. We looked every-where."

Brian walked toward me and held out his hand.

Knowing that Liza had worn the ring, I gave it up reluctantly.

"Who brought this in here?" Brian demanded.

Kids looked at one another suspiciously. Walker wiped the sweat off his brow, and Maggie bit her lip. Mike's face was grim. No one answered Brian's question.

"I want it," Paul said at last. "Give it to me."

"No," Walker said firmly, "it's theater property. Put it where it belongs, Brian."

Brian nodded, then headed for the backstage steps.

I rubbed my palm, thinking. I hadn't felt anything when I held the ring, and there had been no glimmer of blue during this incident. Nor had there been blue light when I smelled my sister's perfume or heard her voice. These incidents were different from my visions and the last two were witnessed by others besides me. I didn't know how to account for them. Was my sister haunting the theater? Or was there a living, breathing person behind these three events? If the latter, someone among us wanted to rattle nerves.

Perhaps someone suspected I was Jenny Montgomery and wanted to unmask me. Or maybe these pranks were aimed at torturing and unmasking another person, the murderer.

What would Liza's murderer do if it was discovered that I was her sister? Till now it hadn't occurred to me that my relationship to her might put me in danger. I would have to be more careful that no one found out.

Tuesday night I went to bed early. My room, where I had feared having more visions, was now my refuge.

Not that I sat in the window anymore. I stretched out in bed and listened to another of Maggie's relaxation tapes, then read until I fell asleep.

The sound of a bell startled me, pulling me out of a dreamless slumber. It was a repeated, echoey sound, like a bell in a school building—a fire alarm! I had to get up, I had to leave, but my arms and legs felt too heavy to lift. I lay there listening to the bell.

"Jenny, come on! Jenny, please!"

Liza reached for my hand. I couldn't see her, but I knew it was she.

"Don't be afraid," she told me, grasping my fingers.

"But I am afraid!"

"I'll help you," she said, her hand tightening around mine.

"Jenny, Jenny, wake up!"

I was shaken hard. Shawna was tugging on my hand, and Maggie was bending over me, her face pale and glistening with sweat.

"It's a fire alarm," Maggie said, raising her voice above the shrill pulsing of the bell. Sirens sounded in the distance. "We have to get out."

Shawna dragged me to my feet.

"Where's the fire?"

"Don't know," said Shawna.

"May be a false alarm," said Maggie. "But go out the window. Go, girls!"

We climbed through in our bare feet and landed softly on the grass below. Maggie followed us and pushed us away from the house, toward the fraternity, where others were gathering. I saw her mouth moving silently: she kept counting heads.

"That's everyone from our place," Lynne assured her.

Guys had come out of the fraternity and kids from the other two houses were arriving, awakened by the sirens. As the first fire engine pulled up in front of the house, Brian joined his mother and us.

"In the kitchen again?" he asked, and I remembered that there had been a small fire at Drama House last year.

"I didn't smell any smoke," Maggie replied.

They headed toward the firefighters to talk to them. Our crowd was growing larger, not just with students but also curious neighbors who had heard the sirens. Keri stood next to Paul, her face flushed slightly. Paul's eyes roved the crowd. Mike stood apart, watching the firefighters who were circling the house. His eyes flicked over to me, studied me for a moment, then shifted away. Brian was at my elbow.

"Everyone okay here?" Brian asked, addressing me and the other girls who were clustered together, but his eyes lingered on me.

We all spoke at the same time, asking him what was going on.

"It's probably a false alarm," Brian told us. "Did you notice anything odd? Did you hear anyone moving around inside the house or creeping around the perimeter?"

I shook my head with the others, and Shawna burst out laughing.

"Didn't hear anything, Jenny?" she teased. "Talk

about waking the dead! From now on I'm keeping a trumpet handy to blow in your ear."

"Did you have trouble waking up?" Brian asked.

"I heard the alarm bell, but it became part of a dream, a dream I couldn't shake off."

He frowned. "What do you mean?"

"I just couldn't wake up."

"Don't worry," Shawna told him. "If it happens again, I won't mess around. She'll be up."

Brian rejoined his mother. Tomas came over and Shawna filled him in on the situation. I sat on the grass next to them, thinking about my dream. I found it scary that a dream could take hold of my mind so powerfully, I could barely break free of it. Even when bells were ringing and someone was shaking me, I had struggled to find my way back to waking life. I felt as if Liza had grasped my mind the way she had clutched my hand in the dream, and she wouldn't let go—not until I found her murderer.

While the firefighters continued to search the building, making sure this was a false alarm, Maggie came over and called all of the students together.

"This is unbelievable," she said, her gray eyes dark with anger. "It is senseless, stupid, and, most of all, dangerous. False alarms make people reluctant to respond quickly the next time they hear an alarm. And when a real fire occurs, thirty seconds can make the difference between life and death.

"It is the policy of Chase College to expel any student found guilty of this kind of dorm prank and to press criminal charges. We know the alarm on the outside of Drama House was pulled. If we find out who did it, you know the consequences. I don't expect it to happen again."

She strode away and everyone exchanged glances.

"Has anyone seen Walker?" Denise asked after a moment of silence.

"No, he lets Maggie take care of this kind of stuff," Katie replied. "She's a natural at lecturing."

"Look, there's that strange custodian guy."

I saw Arthur standing at the edge of the yard, half hidden by a bush, his eyes darting nervously here and there.

"He gives me the creeps," said Lynne.

"Me, too," agreed another girl. "You ever seen how his face twitches? It makes my own skin crawl."

"He's been nice to me," Tomas told them. "He's helped me a lot with setting up scenery."

"Why is he here? He doesn't live on campus, does he?" asked Shawna.

"I bet he pulled the alarm," said Denise. "I bet next time he'll set a fire."

"I bet he's a psychotic murderer," Katie added.

"Maybe he just heard the sirens like everyone else," I suggested.

"Hey, don't ruin our fun, girlfriend," Shawna chided me. "Every camp needs a murderous maniac."

"This camp already had one." As soon as I spoke, I regretted it.

Shawna raised an eyebrow at me, puzzled by the sharpness in my voice. "Okay," she replied with a shrug.

We were finally allowed back in the building. Brian

and his mother continued to talk, while the other R.A.s shepherded their campers back to the dorms. As those of us from Drama House started toward the porch, Arthur cut across the lawn. We reached the steps at the same time, and some of the girls shied to the other side. Shawna and I turned to him.

"Don't trust anyone," Arthur said softly. "Not anyone."

fifteen

Walker must have been told what happened before rehearsal the next morning, but he didn't bring it up. Katie was right: Maggie got stuck with the disciplinary stuff. Given that everyone was short on sleep, rehearsal went amazingly well. The play had been blocked in its entirety, and Walker was talking about our getting off book—getting our lines down—by next week.

During our midmorning break I went downstairs to return a relaxation tape to Maggie and get the next one in the series. Finding her office door closed, I raised my hand to knock, then heard someone speaking.

"You're blowing this way out of proportion," Brian said.

"I don't think so," Maggie replied coolly. "I think it's rather important that a mother be able to trust her son."

"But there was no point in telling you until—"

"It was too late?" she suggested.

"Don't put words in my mouth!"

"Brian, how can I trust that you're not—"

"You just have to," he told her. "I'm better at these things than you are. Let *me* handle the situation, Mom, okay? Okay?"

"She won't," a hushed voice interjected.

I jumped at its closeness. Arthur seemed to have materialized out of nowhere.

"Those two are always fighting," he said, his jaw quickly thrusting out and retracting like a turtle's.

"Parents and kids do," I replied quietly.

"They make me jittery," he went on. "People like that, you don't know what they're going to do."

"What do you mean?"

"People like that just go off suddenly," he said. "I've seen it happen."

I wondered if Arthur knew of some real trouble between Maggie and Brian or if he was projecting on them his own uneasy state of mind.

"Arthur, last night, when we were returning to Drama House, why did you tell us not to trust anyone?"

He didn't answer, just chewed a square yellow fingernail. His clothes smelled smoky. Farther down the hall was the door to the tower. I reasoned that he had slipped in there to have a cigarette, then emerged and surprised me. He probably knew all the nooks and crannies of the theater. According to my mother, it isn't the CIA who knows the secrets of the world, but building custodians and hairdressers.

"Have you worked at Stoddard long?" I asked.

"Long enough," he replied.

"Did you work here last summer? Were you around for last year's camp?"

He shoved nervous hands in his pockets. "No. I move in winter. Winter always makes me feel like I should be somewhere else. I came here last winter."

So he couldn't have observed something suspicious when my sister was killed. But he might have noticed some recent activities that would be useful for me to know.

"When the electricity went off yesterday, were you around?"

"I'm always around," he replied guardedly.

"Oh, I know, I know you do your job. I was just wondering if you saw anyone doing something he or she shouldn't. Or perhaps you saw one of the campers alone in the building, not with the group of us."

"You came back alone on Monday," Arthur noted.

Oh, good. He'd seen *me* being suspicious, and I hadn't even been aware of him.

"Anyone else?"

"Paul and the weird girl."

"Arthur, do you have any idea who could be cutting the power?"

"No," he replied quickly. "I don't know nothing! I don't see nothing!"

"Okay, okay, no problem, I was just wondering."

He was too nervous and worried to provide information now, and the best thing for me to do was back off. But I had been around a lot of custodians in my life; I would slowly make him my friend.

"Where are we going?" I asked, two hours later.

"If it were up to me, California," Brian said, taking my lunch tray from me, setting it down at the base of a maple at the far end of the quadrangle. "But that's a long walk, so let's stop here."

The energy our troupe had shown earlier in the day had run out by lunchtime. Maggie didn't want kids returning to the dorms unsupervised, but she let us bring our lunches out on the quad and take a nap there, where she could keep an eye on us. Kids had scattered over the grass, some in the shade of tall, leafy trees, others basking in the sun.

Brian stretched out on the grass. I sat and rested my back against the maple's rough bark.

"The truth is, Jenny, there are two more long days till the weekend. Lots of stupid stuff is happening around here, and I have to deal with it. I need a reward—lunch with you."

"It must be tough for you and your mother. Being in charge of the dorms as well as working all day in the theater, you never get a break."

"I think it's getting to her more than me," he said.

"How so?"

Lying on his back, Brian gazed up at the tree, thinking before he answered. The movement of the branches, the shifting sun and shade, were reflected in his dark eyes. "She's overreacting to things. The pranks in the theater have got her really upset. This morning she accused me of them."

I decided not to tell him I'd heard part of their argument. "Why does she think you'd do something like that?"

"To mess things up. To get back at Walker."

"I didn't realize you disliked him that much."

"I don't. I know I'm a good actor, a good stage manager, too, and let what he says run off me. But I think his criticism of me over the years has gotten to my mother. She tries to act professional and doesn't let people see what upsets her, but she's pretty sensitive. She can get down about stuff, really down, and she imagines I feel the same as she does."

"Do you have any idea who could be behind these pranks?" I asked. I was not about to mention my first theory that Liza was haunting us. I knew Brian was too practical to consider it.

"Paul, but I don't have proof. Paul and someone else who can cut the electricity, maybe Arthur, someone not expected to be present when my mother counts heads."

"Does Paul have a case against Walker?"

"Not really. Walker has given him a lot of breaks." Brian rolled on his side and pulled himself up on his elbow. "I don't know if I should say this. I could be way off, but I think Paul does the pranks as a way of making Liza Montgomery live on."

I thought of how Paul sniffed at her perfume, as if he couldn't get enough of it. My stomach felt queasy and I set down my sandwich.

"Is something wrong?"

"No."

Brian sat up. "Jenny, I have to tell you something. It may sound crazy, but I have a feeling it won't."

I met his eyes warily. "All right."

"This morning, when I was talking with my mother, I remembered a conversation I had last summer with Liza Montgomery. I remembered that Liza had a sister named Jenny."

I looked away.

"According to Liza, Jenny knew a lot about theater, and she had talent, but she was afraid to get up on stage. She never did any acting."

"No," I said quietly, "she did gymnastics."

I heard his quick intake of breath. He rested his hand on mine. "Why did you come here?" he asked. "It has got to be miserable for you."

"I told her I'd come. I promised Liza I'd visit her. I just"—my voice caught in my throat—"arrived a little late."

He lifted his hand and touched my cheek gently. "I'm sorry. I'm really sorry about what happened."

I nodded, pressing my lips together, hoping he wouldn't hear the sob building in my throat. He leaned closer and brushed my hair back from my face.

"There is something else I want to know, but I'll ask when you're feeling better."

"Ask now," I said.

He waited a minute, until I was breathing more regularly. "Does anyone here know who you are?"

I shook my head.

"You're sure?"

"There would be no reason for them to know. I don't look like Liza or act like her, and most people, like you, wouldn't expect me to come here after what happened. I love Liza with all my heart, but, as you probably noticed, she was a person who spent a lot of time thinking and talking about herself. I'm sure she bragged about Dad, but truthfully, I'm surprised you ever heard she had a sister."

"It came up once, in a conversation about the pros and cons of being involved with theater when your parents are. That's something Liza and I shared. But, Jenny, don't you see, if I heard your name and finally made the connection, somebody else might."

"I suppose."

"Does Mike know?"

"I'm sure he doesn't." If Mike had figured it out, he wouldn't have lied to me about his relationship to Liza.

"It worries me," Brian continued. "Because if Mike knows, Paul knows—they're close. And Paul was totally obsessed with Liza, still is. If he finds out you're her sister, he might . . ." His voice trailed off.

"What?" I asked.

I thought he was going to answer, then he changed his mind. "I don't know. My imagination's working overtime."

"Brian, have you ever thought that Liza might have been killed by someone other than the serial murderer?"

"I guess everyone here looked at everyone else when we first heard about her death. But then we learned that the murder had the trademark of the serial killer who was working his way up the East Coast."

"Which doesn't mean anything," I replied. "Imitating the style of others is something theater people do very well."

"What do you mean?" he asked. "Do you suspect someone?"

"I'm mulling over the possibility."

Brian's face grew worried. "Jenny, I think you should leave."

"Not yet."

"Before anyone else figures out who you are."

"I can't. Not until the dreams stop."

"What dreams?" he asked.

I knew better than to say I was having psychic visions. "I keep dreaming of Liza. It's as if she is trying to tell me something."

His eyebrows drew together. His mouth got the same determined look as his mother's. "I'm trying to tell you something, with no *as if*. You need to get out of here."

I shook my head stubbornly.

"Listen to me, Jenny. Paul's room is like a shrine to your sister. Sometimes I'm not sure he knows she is dead. It's as if a switch suddenly flips inside his brain, and he can't tell real from unreal."

Brian detached a set of keys from his belt. "This is my master key," he said, pulling it off the ring. "It opens all the doors in the frat. This afternoon, when you're not rehearsing and everyone else is occupied, I'll send you on a fake errand. I want you to go to Paul's room and see for yourself. Second floor. His name's on the door."

I gazed at the brass key Brian dropped in my hand.

"No, it isn't ethical," he added as if he'd read my thoughts, "and I don't care. All I care about is you seeing what you're dealing with." He took my face in his hands. "Believe me, Jenny, I don't want you to go. New York is a long way from here. But I think you're taking big chances."

"I'm not ready to leave yet."

"This afternoon ought to make you ready." He let go and glanced around. "We'd better eat."

We gulped down our food and Maggie called everyone in. Brian returned my tray and his to the cafeteria, sending me ahead to the theater. I joined Tomas and Shawna at the back of a crowd filing into Stoddard. Too late I noticed that Mike was in front of them. I fussed with my backpack and pretended not to see him.

"Hello," Mike said cheerfully.

I hoped he was speaking to someone else.

"Hello, Jenny. Is anyone home?"

Shawna and Tomas laughed at his question.

I glanced up. "Hi."

"Did you have a nice lunch?" he asked.

Had he been watching? I wondered.

"We were going to join you," Shawna said, her eyes bright with teasing, "but Tomas said it looked like a tree-for-two, so we didn't."

Tomas gave a little shrug and smile, then followed Shawna into the building. Mike stayed behind and caught me with a light hand before I could enter. He stood close, his neck and shoulders blocking out the light, making me acutely aware of his size and strength. When I glanced up at his face, I saw his eyes following a trickle of sweat down my neck.

"For a moment during lunch," he said, "I was afraid you were going to have another accident."

My cheeks got hot. "Must have been a pretty boring lunch," I replied. "I hope your dinner is better."

sixteen

*S*oon after we came back from our three o'clock break, Brian handed me a diagram of the play's revised set and sent me off to "make copies." I circled Stoddard then headed toward the fraternity.

The house's design was almost identical to that of Drama House, but the peeling gray paint on the outside and its dilapidated condition inside made it seem like a very different place. The foyer was painted dark purple, its only light a bare bulb dangling from the ceiling. The stairway's banister, also purple, had deep gashes in it, and several of its balusters were missing.

I set the folder Brian had given me on the steps, then continued upstairs and found the door to Paul's room. Only then did I hesitate. I was invading his privacy, and I wasn't sure the private part of Paul's life was something I wanted to know. But I had to do this, for Liza's sake and my own. I slipped the key in the hole.

As soon as I opened the door, I smelled the perfume, Liza's perfume. Then I saw the pictures. She was everywhere, on the bureau and desk, hanging inside the mirror frame, taped to all four walls, her face large as life in some of the photos. I felt as if I'd walked inside a house of mirrors with my sister. Her image and perfume overwhelmed me, and I reached for a desk chair to sit down.

Turning slowly in the chair, I studied the photos one by one. Many I had never seen before and must have been taken at camp. Since Paul didn't occupy this room during the college year, he had brought them back with him. Why did he surround himself with these pictures? Perhaps for the same reason that Brian believed he played the pranks: to keep Liza "alive." But was it obsessive love which made him try to keep her alive, or the need to deny that something terrible had occurred?

My eyes scanned the surface of the battered desk, then stopped. I picked up two pens and scribbled with them on my palm, leaving bright green and pink marks. Guys didn't usually write with those colors, but Liza had loved to. I opened the desk drawer and spotted a pink address book. I checked the entries, but I already knew it was Liza's. Then I saw her turquoise hair clip. It was as if my sister were living here!

I pushed back from the desk and walked around the room. The bookshelves had photos of Liza, but nothing else belonging to her. I stopped at the bureau. Liza's watch. I held it gently, then closed my hand around it. We had found Liza's other watch at home, which meant my vision was accurate: a third watch, one that didn't belong to her, had been fastened to her wrist.

I wanted this one back, and I wanted her hair clip, her address book, her pens, even the photos that had not been ours. I hated the thought of Paul's eyes roving over the image of her face, his narrow fingers touching her belongings, but I had to leave everything where I found it.

I set down the watch and noticed the shimmer of an object half hidden by a computer game magazine with a lurid red cover. Lifting the magazine, I found my sister's bracelet, the wide silver bangle I had given her for her sixteenth birthday. I picked it up and slid it over my hand.

The moment the silver touched my wrist I felt its icy sting. Cold traveled up my arm and fear rippled through me, wrapping my heart in a chilling web. Paul's room slipped into shadow, then darkness, its edges glimmering blue. I could smell the creek.

Not again! I thought. Please, don't make me go through it again!

I yanked the bracelet over my knuckles and heard it land on the bureau. The blue glint disappeared and the darkness of my vision frayed until the sunlit room shone through again. But fear still made my heart beat fast; Liza's fear throbbed inside me.

I held my head with my hands, trying to sort out what was happening. Most of my sister's belongings, such as her pens and hair clip, did not affect me when I touched them. It was as if the emotion coursing through her the night she died had imprinted certain things she touched—the window she had climbed through to meet Mike, the bank beneath the bridge, a piling beneath the pavilion—enough so that when I touched them they could engender my visions. Liza's extreme fear and pain the moment she was murdered had charged the hammer even more. Feeling the same sensation when I touched the bracelet, I wondered if she had been wearing it when she died.

I looked quickly inside Paul's bureau and closet and probably should have searched further, but I had seen all I could endure for the moment. After placing the magazine so that it partially covered the bracelet—I didn't dare touch the bangle again—I checked that everything else was as I had found it, then left and locked the door. Heading toward the stairway, I noticed Mike's name on the door across the hall.

I didn't try to rationalize my snooping, but simply unlocked the door and let myself in. Mike was neater than Paul, though his concept of order appeared to be leaving everything out and stacking his belongings in thematic piles. Clothes, books, CDs, tennis balls, sunscreen and shaving lotion—all of it in organized piles—covered the tops of his desk, bureau, and chair. Glancing down at a stack of books, I noticed a satiny edge of paper protruding from the pages of one. A photograph. Curious, I pulled it out.

It caught me completely by surprise. Liza and I, our arms around each other's shoulders, wearing T-shirts made in honor of our father, laughed into the camera's eye. It was a favorite photo of my sister's because, as she used to say, "We look just like us!"

Mike knew who I was. He had known from the start. But if he knew my identity, why had he lied to me about his and Liza's relationship? Did he fear I would pepper him with questions until he revealed something he didn't want me to know?

I slipped the photo back in the book. I had seen what Brian wanted me to see, and then some, but the more I knew, the less I understood.

Walker ended rehearsal early that day, reminding us that it was Movie Night. Kids left the theater quickly, and Walker followed Maggie down to the offices. Both had been edgy that afternoon; according to Shawna, they had argued fiercely while I was gone on my errand. Brian followed them downstairs, hoping, he said, to get them to cool it.

I had already returned the master key to him, choosing a time when there were too many people around for us to confer. I didn't want to discuss what I had discovered.

Tomas and I were about to leave the set when Arthur and another guy from maintenance arrived, carrying the extension ladder that Tomas had been calling about all day. The two men made a hasty exit, perhaps afraid of being asked to do something else. After several clumsy efforts Tomas and I managed to rest the ladder against the catwalk thirty feet up.

"Shall I give it a try?" I asked.

Tomas shook his head. "I'd rather have a couple people here holding it."

"Don't worry. I'm not going far."

Tomas held the ladder and I started up the aluminum rungs. On the sixth one I stopped. I didn't like the give of the ladder, the way it vibrated in my hands and the metallic noise it made.

"Everything okay?" Tomas asked, pulling his head back to look at me.

"You're going to have to find someone else for the job," I said, climbing back down.

"I've already got them lined up."

"Shall we store this on its side?" I asked.

"No." He gestured toward a table full of tools and the bolt of blue fabric. "I'd like to get the sky hung right away tomorrow."

"Walker might get irritable if he starts the day with a ladder in the middle of his stage."

"If he does, I'll say I'm sorry," Tomas replied.

"I see. Better to say you're sorry later, than ask for permission before?"

He smiled. "Sometimes, with some people, yes."

"Tomas, you continually surprise me."

We gathered our belongings and walked back to the dorms together, passing Mike, who was carrying a tennis racket and a can of balls. He said hello, more to Tomas than me, and continued on. After Tomas and I parted, I headed in the direction Mike had taken, figuring there were courts somewhere beyond the Stoddard parking area and athletic fields.

I found him playing alone, hitting a tennis ball against a wall in a practice court, driving it hard. *Thump! Thump!* A day's worth of heat radiated from the pavement, and the humidity wrung every last degree from the lowering sun. Mike's shirt was soaked through and his forearms shone with sweat, still he played on as if some demon were goading him. Sometimes he slammed the ball hard, too hard to get the rebound—that seemed to give him the most satisfaction.

He didn't notice when I sat on a bench outside the court's wire fence. I brushed the gnats away from my face and waited. At last he stopped to drink from a water bottle.

"May I talk to you?"

He spun around, surprised, then glanced about to see if anyone else was there. "All right," he said, but he stayed where he was, midcourt on the other side of the tall wire fence. "About what?"

"My sister."

He didn't move.

"My sister Liza."

He wiped his face on his shirt and walked toward me, but only as far as the fence, keeping it between us.

"When did you know who I was?" I asked.

"As soon as I saw you."

"Why didn't you say something?"

"Why didn't you?"

"I have reasons," I replied.

"So do I."

I kicked at the grass, frustrated. He turned the face of his racket horizontal and bounced the ball against the court.

"Why did Liza give you the picture of her and me?"

"I guess she told you I liked it," he said, continuing to dribble the ball. Then his hand swooped down and snatched it. "No, she couldn't have, or you would have realized that I recognized you. How do you know about the photo?"

"I saw it in your room this afternoon."

"In my room?" His eyes narrowed, turning the color of blue slate. "What were you doing there?"

"Snooping."

He looked at me, amazed. "I can't believe it," he said. "I can't believe you'd do something like that."

"At least I'm honest in admitting it. You lied to me about Liza."

He turned his back on me and drove the ball hard against the wall. "You lied the day you introduced yourself as Jenny Baird."

"If you knew who I was, why did you lie to me about her?" I persisted.

He faced me again, frowning.

"Why didn't you admit you were dating, in love, whatever?"

"Whatever," he echoed.

"You had to realize she'd tell me about the two of you. Sisters share almost everything."

"I don't know what Liza told you, but we were just friends."

I shook my head and turned to walk away.

"Jenny, listen. I may have . . . misled Liza," he said haltingly.

I glanced back.

"When we first got to camp we became friends almost instantly. We spent a lot of time together and told each other stuff about our families. We had a lot in common—I mean, our dream of being actors and all. I realized too late that Liza was misinterpreting things, that she thought I was interested in her romantically when really I was–" He broke off.

I stepped toward the fence and finished his statement: "Interested in my father, interested in his connections. Maybe he could get you a scholarship, like Walker did," I said and started to laugh, though I didn't think the situation funny. "You know, I've been used by guys who wanted to date my sister. I've been used by theater groupies who wanted access to Dad, but I didn't think something like that would ever happen to Liza."

Mike said nothing.

"Do you have any idea how much it hurts to be used that way–how much it makes you feel like a nothing?"

"I tried to let her down easy. I tried to back out, but she wouldn't let go."

"Did you kiss her?" I blurted.

He looked at me curiously. "Does it make any difference to you?"

"No, of course not." Talking about lying, I thought, I had just told a big one.

Mike was silent for a moment. "Well, as you know, accidents happen."

I stared at him angrily. "Next time, kiss up to my father, not me and my sister."

He took a step back.

"Why did you send Liza the note asking her to meet you by the river?"

"I didn't."

"You know what note I mean," I went on.

"The one Keri claims she saw, asking Liza to meet me at the gazebo. If there was one, I didn't send it. And, besides, Liza was killed under the bridge."

"Under the pavilion," I corrected him.

His forehead creased. "They found her under the bridge."

"She was murdered under the pavilion."

"How do you know that?" he asked.

"I"—I was reluctant to tell him about the visions—"I sense it."

He moved closer. "Sense it how?"

I was tired of lying. "I have dreams about it, visions."

"Like the dreams you had when you were a little girl? The blue dreams?"

I blinked. "How do you know about them?"

"Liza told me. She said that sometimes you would dream the same thing as she. She thought you had a special connection to her, that you were telepathic."

I grasped the fence, twisting my fingers around the wire.

"She talked to me about you all the time," Mike said. "She really missed you. I was so sure you'd come to see her."

"Well, I have—finally." I fought back the tears.

From the other side of the fence Mike smoothed the tips of my fingers with his. "Why did you come? Why now?"

I pulled my hand free of the fence. I didn't want to get into that with him. "Does Paul know who I am? Does Keri or Walker? Did you tell them?"

"I haven't told anyone," he said. "Have you?"

"Just Brian. Who is playing the pranks?"

"Until yesterday, I suspected Brian—Brian with some help from Arthur," he added. "Both would enjoy messing up Walker's rehearsals."

"Brian says it's Paul."

"That's possible. The ring that Liza wore for last year's production, the one that rolled across the floor yesterday, was taken by Keri. Kids thought it was misplaced, but she took it last year and gave it to Paul."

"I don't understand. Why would Keri give Paul something connected to Liza when she was so jealous of her?"

He shrugged. "Maybe Keri hoped Paul would be grateful to her, that he would be grateful and notice her."

"That doesn't make sense."

Mike smiled. "I guess you've never been in love with someone who's in love with someone else. You find yourself saying and doing stupid things just to get that person to look at you."

I looked away. "Does Paul know much about sound equipment?"

"He's pretty good with that stuff when he puts his mind to it. Why?"

"The first day of camp, when you were in the theater, up in the balcony, did you hear voices, voices that sounded like Liza's?"

"All I heard was you saying Liza's lines."

"Before that."

"I came in right then," he said.

At least he kept his story consistent.

"Well, I heard voices. The sound, like Liza's perfume and the sudden appearance of her ring, was haunting, but I believe it was simply a recording of Liza's voice overlapping itself."

"So these pranks are directed at you?"

I shook my head. "I don't think so. I'm beginning to think I stumbled into a private rehearsal. It would have been a good time for the person behind the pranks to practice, since everyone was supposed to be busy with check-in at the dorms. If I did barge into a rehearsal, then these hauntings were planned before camp began, before anyone had a chance to recognize me. And I'm sure no one thought I'd be coming."

"I didn't think I would come this year," Mike said. "But then I found that I had to in order to go on. Is it like that for you? Is that why you came?"

He kept wanting an answer to that question. "It was at first."

"And now?"

"Liza wants me to find her murderer."

His eyes widened.

"She told me, sort of," I added lamely.

"But the serial killer could be anywhere."

"I believe she was killed by someone who knew her, then doctored the crime to make it look like part of the series."

He was silent for a long moment, spinning the tennis racket in his hand. "That's why you were searching my room. You think I'm involved."

"I think more than one person is involved and that more than one person knows something."

"I can't believe you'd think that I—"

"I have to. I can't trust anyone."

"Including Brian?" he prodded.

"Until I know more, everyone is a suspect, everyone but Liza and me."

seventeen

I left Mike beating balls against the wall and returned to Drama House. The common room was air-conditioned, but after washing my face, I chose the quiet and drowsy warmth of my own room.

I set my alarm, hoping to nap, but I couldn't fall asleep. My mind was restless, full of questions and suspicions, flicking from one theory to the next, as if I were clicking buttons on an Internet site. *Uncle Louie*, I remembered suddenly, and opened my laptop to check my e-mail.

His reply to my letter came up on the screen. It was typical Uncle Louie.

Greetings, my most beautiful goddaughter!

What a pleasure to hear from you—even if it was not to invite me to the camp performance. I could make all kinds of pleasant chitchat here, but as I know that you are a young lady who keeps to a schedule, let me hasten to the question at hand, the history of Walker Burke.

I cannot be entirely negative toward Walker; after all, he did give Broadway the finest star we have today, inviting your father to America. Walker offered your father his first role in New York, and it was quite a nice showcase for his talents. He found him his second job as well.

The problem with Walker was that even as the years went by and your father's skills far exceeded any opportunities Walker had given him, he felt your father owed him. Perhaps your father felt so, too, for he agreed to star in a new play, a script and production about which I had many doubts. To begin with, the producer was in love with the writer—you know how romance clouds the vision—and he was desperate to please her. Meanwhile, Walker was desperate to establish himself as a Broadway director. He even put in some money of his own—not much by theater standards, but probably his life savings, given his status at that point.

I believe your father knew the play was a dud well before previews. Opening night reviews ran from mediocre to bad. Nevertheless, Lee performed for another two weeks, and because of his name, they brought in a full house each night. Walker, the writer, and the producer were quite pleased with the production; not so your father, who dropped out the third week. The play sank faster than the *Titanic*.

Walker, having lost his money and his reputa-
tion, was furious and blamed everything on your
father. Eventually he left New York and, apparently, beached in Maryland. Too bad he can't let
go of the past; old grudges and bitterness always
hurt the individual more than the one whom he
believes injured him.

So ends today's lesson. (What a dutiful godfather I am, not only answering your question but
imparting that last bit of wisdom!) I hope you are
finding the camp enjoyable, and I know you are
finding it challenging. I am inexpressibly proud of
you for taking this on, knowing your reluctance in
the past.

Do let this old man know when the performance will be.

                              Love,
                              Uncle Louie

I leaned back against the slats of my desk chair,
thinking about Walker, realizing that he had plenty reason to hate my father. Uncle Louie told the story from
his perspective, the same perspective as my father's, but
if I imagined Brian with all his ambition working to
make it in L.A., or Mike with his intense love for theater struggling to make it in New York, I could easily
understand how Walker had felt. His big chance had
come, the theater was full every night, then the whole
thing came crashing down. Years of dreams and effort
ended with my father's one decision.

Uncle Louie was right about a grudge hurting the

one who bore it, but it didn't *always* hurt that person more—not if he acted on it, not if he suddenly got a chance to lash out at someone close to the person he begrudged—say someone as close as a child.

The Merchant of Venice was the film being shown that night. Usually, Lawrence Olivier mesmerized me, but tonight Walker held my attention. I watched him out of the corner of my eye, trying to tell if he was absorbed in the movie or simply sitting through it. At eight-thirty, with another forty-five minutes of film to go, I headed to the ladies' room and continued out the door of the Student Union. My plan was to search Walker's files and return to the darkened auditorium just before the final credits.

I wasn't sure what I was looking for, but I planned to start with student files—mine and, if he still had it, Liza's, as well as anything he kept on Paul, Keri, Mike, and Brian. One little notation made by Walker or one tiny fact from a person's application might shed light on how he or someone else could have the mind and the means to kill my sister.

The back entrance of Stoddard was open as usual. I wondered what time campus security locked the building for the night. I'd have a lot of explaining to do if an officer caught me. I walked silently down the hall toward Walker's office, turned the corner, and tried his door. It was locked.

On to Plan B, the window, I thought, and exited the building as quietly as I'd come. Since Walker's office was at the corner, its ground-level windows would be the first set facing the quadrangle. It was an exposed area, but it was nearly dark now, just a glimmer of mauve showing in the western sky, and Stoddard's outside lights were clustered at its front and back entrances. With all the campers in the Student Union, the quad was deserted.

Then I noticed light coming from a window the next office down—Maggie's. She hadn't been at the movie, and I had hoped that Walker, realizing that she was working too hard, had given her the evening off. Maybe I could tell her I'd left something in Walker's office and ask her to let me in, I thought. But that wouldn't give me enough time to search. I turned back to Walker's window.

It was paned and half the height of a normal window, its lower sill even with the grass. Gently but firmly I pushed up against the cross braces. The window slid open. I pulled off my shoes, squeezed through, and dropped four feet down to the floor. After shutting the window I pulled the blinds and turned on a desk lamp, figuring that its light would be dimmer than the overhead and draw less attention. I set my shoes by the window so I wouldn't forget them.

There were two large file cabinets in Walker's office. I tiptoed to them and tried one, then the other, but both were locked. I remembered that during the day Walker carried a ring of keys, but used a single key attached to a small leather pouch to open his office. I figured he kept his collection of theater keys here at work and glanced around the room—files, bookcases, pots with dead plants, another bookcase, a cluttered desk. I tried the desk drawers. In the bottom one I found the ring of keys.

It occurred to me that this was how Paul and Keri had gotten into the tower. Walker was always tossing the ring down somewhere. It wouldn't be hard to slip off a key and get it duplicated at a hardware store. Gradually a person could gain access to all kinds of rooms and storage places in the theater, which would be very helpful if one were haunting it.

It didn't take long to figure out which of the slender keys on the ring fitted the locks of the file cabinets. I eased open the top drawer of one and found a set of binders—prompt books for plays Walker had directed in the past. The next drawer down had student records. I tabbed through them, but they were files for students who attended the college, not summer camp. The drawer below that had teaching materials, exams and syllabi. I knelt on the floor to look at the files in the bottom drawer.

The folders contained a curious hodgepodge of stuff, technical drawings of the stage and light equipment, old costume catalogs, old scripts, warranties for coffeepots, hair dryers, and drills, and, at the back of the cabinet, a file without a label. I opened it with one finger, just enough to glance at its contents—newspaper articles. BRIDGE KILLER STRIKES AGAIN a headline read. I plucked out the file and opened it.

The clipping on top was an account of the murder that had occurred in South Carolina, two months after the one in Florida. Filed behind it were shorter articles that had been gathered off the Internet, reports on both the first and second murder. There were a dozen articles about the third killing, the one in Virginia, which confirmed the police's fear that they had a serial murderer on their hands. In all of the articles certain details, like the smashed watches, the position of the bodies under the bridges, and the condition of the victims' clothes were highlighted in yellow, along with various theories about the kind of person who would do something like this. There was nothing about my sister's murder or the one in New Jersey; all the information Walker had wanted was gathered before she died.

I slipped the file under my arm. It proved nothing more than an unusual interest in learning the details and style of these murders; still, it was something to show the police, who were unlikely to believe a teen's visions.

I checked the files in the next cabinet and found this year's campers near the bottom. In mine there was nothing but my application form, essays, and recommendations. I hunted for Paul's, then glanced at my watch and realized that in trying to be quiet I had used up a lot of time. I wanted to get back to the movie before the lights came on. I closed the final drawer and stood up quickly, carelessly knocking over a wastebasket. In the silence of the building the roll of the metal basket sounded like crashing cymbals. I wondered whether to lie low or rush to the window. If Maggie looked out hers, she might catch me climbing out. I clicked off the lamp.

"Walker?" Maggie called. "Is that you?"

I flattened myself against the wall, not sure what

could be seen through the frosted glass. I heard her footsteps approaching. "Walker?"

I figured it would be easier to explain my presence to her than to security. But then, security was so lax around here, it might take an officer forever to get here. Better to go through the window, I thought. Then I heard keys rattling on the other side of the door and knew Maggie was about to open it. I did instead.

"Jenny!" she exclaimed. "What are you doing here?"

She looked tired, not just in her eyes but in the sag of her shoulders.

"I was looking for something."

"What?" she asked, clicking on the overhead light, eyeing the folder tucked under my arm.

I opened the file for her. "I found this in Walker's cabinet. Look—these are articles about the serial killings, the first three, not the one that happened last year. Why would he have something like this?"

She took the folder from me and paged slowly through the articles. "Probably because he wants to try dinner theater next spring, to stage one of those popular murder mysteries that involve the audience. Walker always does research, collecting details from nonfiction accounts of whatever subject or historical period is being dealt with in a play."

I bit my lip. I wasn't convinced.

"Now, Jenny, I have a question for you. Why are you sneaking around in here?"

"I've got a good reason," I said, then paused, trying to decide how much to tell her and where to begin.

"I'm waiting."

"It's complicated."

She glanced at her watch, then handed me the folder. "Put this back where you found it and come to my office. We'll walk over to the Student Union, and you can explain on the way."

I returned the folder to the cabinet, picked up the trash can, and slipped on my shoes. When I rejoined Maggie, I found her standing next to a bookcase, leaning on it, her head in her hands.

"Maggie, are you all right?"

Her head lifted quickly. "Yes, fine."

"You don't look fine," I observed.

She walked over to her desk and sat down wearily. "I'm just hungry. I haven't eaten all day. And I'm a bit down," she admitted.

"You work too many hours," I said. "You need more time for yourself. You can't always be worrying about drama camp."

"My work is my relief," she replied. "If that was all I had to deal with, my life would be wonderful."

"What do you mean?"

She fidgeted with her scarf. "I've discovered that Brian is lying to me."

"About what?" I asked.

"It's a serious matter, not one I can discuss with you."

Was this about the pranks, I wondered, or was there something more going on?

Maggie leaned forward on her desk, resting her face on her hands. She looked gray.

"Is there anything I can do for you?"

"No. Why don't you run ahead. We'll talk later."

"I'll get you something to eat," I offered. "They're serving sandwiches after the movie. I'll get one and be right back."

She glanced up at me, rubbing her mouth against her knuckle.

"Just rest here, okay? I'll be back," I told her, hurrying out of her office before she could protest. When I reached the Student Union, the movie had ended and kids were picking up sandwiches. Brian was talking to Walker, both of them laughing over something Brian had said.

I knew that Maggie was a worrier and, at the moment, exhausted. When people are tired, problems and fears become exaggerated. But what if Brian *wasn't* trustworthy? What if he leaked my identity and my purpose for being here? I remembered his description of the way people worked: in the end, everyone is out for himself, he had said, and sometimes that makes people seem for you, and sometimes it makes them seem against you.

"Where did you go, Jenny?"

I jumped and Tomas looked at me curiously. "Didn't mean to scare you," he said. He had two large sandwiches on his plate.

"I was at Stoddard talking to Maggie. She's pretty upset, Tomas, and hasn't eaten all day. May I have one of your sandwiches to take back to her?"

"Sure. Want me to come with you?"

"No."

He handed me the paper plate with the untouched sandwich. "People keep disappearing," he said. "You, Mike, Paul."

I glanced around. "Did Mike and Paul come back?"

"Haven't seen them. I can't figure out why Walker isn't saying anything about it."

Perhaps, I thought, because the two of them were doing something for him.

"Maybe because he leaves that kind of stuff to Maggie," I said aloud. "She's waiting for me back at her office. Catch up with you later, okay?"

Tomas looked puzzled. "Okay."

I hurried back to the theater and let myself in the back door. When I reached Maggie's office, both her door and Walker's were closed, but her light was still on.

"Just me," I said, tapping lightly on the glass.

She didn't respond to my voice or to a harder knock, so I opened the door. She was gone. I walked over to her desk to set down her food and saw a note lying on the seat of her chair. I picked it up to read.

I'm sorry, Brian. I can't go on.
I can't try anymore.
My will is with the lawyer.
Everything should be in order.

I stared at the short sentences, their meaning sinking in slowly. It was a suicide note.

"Maggie?" I called. "Maggie!"

I rushed out of her office, then stopped, not knowing which way to turn. There were too many rooms in this place for me to check them all quickly. And she might not even be in the building. Get Brian, I thought. No, call security to get people to search the building and send the police to her house.

I turned back to make the calls, then spotted her scarf on the floor, halfway down the hall. I noticed the door at the far end was open. The tower door! I ran toward it, hoping I wouldn't be too late.

eighteen

"Maggie!" I shouted from the bottom of the iron stairs. "Maggie, I have to talk to you!"

I thought I heard movement far above me and hurried up the steps. "Maggie, listen to me. Things will get better. I'll help you. I'll find someone who knows how to help you."

I climbed as fast as I could, turning every five steps to rush up the next five, panicking that I wouldn't get there in time. I was out of breath from calling to her. It seemed as if I'd climbed a hundred stories. Just four, I told myself, the four stories of Stoddard. Then the walls began to narrow. I figured I was entering the top of the brick portion of the tower, the area with the shingled roof that was surmounted by the clock.

The stairs became a spiral here, worming their way up through the shrinking space, then on through an area with narrow platforms and square casements containing the clockworks, one facing each direction. The triangular steps were difficult to climb, so narrow on the inside, my feet slipped off. The spiral became a simple ladder to a trapdoor. It was dark, but I felt a splash of night air coming from above. I climbed through the open door and found myself in a space like a covered porch, enclosed by three-foot walls with a pillar at each corner and a roof.

Maggie was sitting sideways inside one of the four bays, her feet drawn up on the sill, her arms wrapped tightly around her knees. Her body shook. I was sure she heard me, but she kept her head turned away from me. If she rolled to the right, she would fall six stories.

"Maggie," I said softly, "I saw your note."

She turned her head jerkily. In the darkness the pupils of her eyes were large. Her mouth trembled.

The tower was no more than five feet across, but I was afraid to move toward her too quickly. If I reached for her suddenly, she might panic and fall.

"I can help you."

"You?" The laughter that spilled from her jangled out of tune.

"I'll find someone to help. Let's go down now."

"No one can help me," she said, her voice pitching high. "I can never get back what I've lost!"

"You mean Brian? You mean your trust in him?"

She laughed again, and this time it was my nerves that jangled. Something was terribly wrong.

"Tell me what's going on," I persisted. "Tell me and maybe I can figure a way—"

"There is no way out for you."

I replayed her disquieting words in my head, confused.

She lowered her feet to the floor and took two steps toward me, extending her arms, reaching to touch my hair. "Such a pretty girl," she said. "And a nice girl, not like your sister."

"Brian told you who I am."

"Such a shame."

She toyed with my hair, making me increasingly nervous. When she touched my cheek, I flinched.

"You shouldn't have come here, Jenny. Liza is gone. What were you looking for?"

"Peace."

Maggie stroked my face with a thumb that felt like cold sandpaper. "Don't you know, there is no peace for those who have lost someone too soon. I still hear Melanie calling me. In the middle of the night I awaken and hear her. *Don't forget me, Mommy. Don't forget,* she says, just as she did when I'd work long hours away from home. In the middle of the night I feel her soft breath on my cheek. Sometimes she tells me what to do."

"What to do—like what?" I asked warily. Maggie was acting strange but not necessarily suicidal. I wondered if she had written the note to lure me up here.

She tilted her head and gazed at me solemnly. "It shouldn't surprise anyone, Jenny, that you became upset at camp. You kept hearing about Liza. You were having dreams about her. And someone was playing pranks, haunting the theater like the ghost of Liza. No wonder you became confused and depressed."

"I am not depressed."

"How unfortunate your parents chose this time to leave you alone." Her voice had shifted from high pitch to low and smooth as syrup. "I'll write a note explaining—in your handwriting, just like that on your application. I'll explain why you had to kill yourself."

I took a step back from her. The strange, sympathetic look on Maggie's face chilled me to the bone. I glanced at the stone sill, then beyond it. Below me the tower roof sloped far too steeply to stop a fall. I began edging toward the trapdoor.

Maggie saw the movement and lunged at me, shoving me back against the wall with such force I couldn't stay on my feet. I slid onto the sill. My head snapped back, as if someone had pulled a chair out from behind me sixty feet up. I reached out wildly for something—anything I could get my hands on—the stone sill, the pillar. My feet touched cement again and I dropped down in a crouch. As long as I was lower than the sill, she couldn't push me over it. I crawled toward the trapdoor.

"Get up! Get up!" Maggie shrieked and kicked at my stomach, bringing her foot up hard into my ribs. Breathless from the blows, I scrambled through the door, dropping down so quickly my foot missed the rung. It caught two rungs down. I descended as fast as I dared. When I reached the spiral stairs, I turned so I could run down them face forward. I heard Maggie's footsteps above me.

At last I was on the regular-size treads. I raced downward. Too fast! My heel slipped over the edge of one. I went sliding down on my back, my left wrist bent behind me. I was stopped by the wall. Pain crippled my left wrist. With my right hand I quickly grasped the railing, pulled myself to my feet, and continued downward.

Reaching the hall, I rushed through it and around the corner toward the back door of the theater. I pushed hard against the double doors. They gave slightly, then stopped. I glanced down at the handle. A chain, someone had chained the doors!

I didn't know what to think. This was the entrance I had come through just a few minutes ago and now it was locked from the inside. Maggie had acted as if she alone was after me, but this door had been chained by someone else.

I heard Maggie's footsteps in the hall and hurried up the steps to the stage. The light above the staircase suddenly went off.

"Who's there?" Maggie called out.

I glanced over my shoulder. The lights in the hall below had also gone off. The uncertainty in Maggie's voice told me she hadn't been the one to cut the power. I tried to remember if I had seen an unmarked door downstairs. If I knew where the electrical room was, I'd have some idea where the other person was, perhaps the person who had chained the doors. But my mind was reeling with fear and the sudden darkness confused me. It must have confused Maggie, too, for I heard doors opening and closing below and soft cries of surprise.

Tiptoeing onto the back of the stage, I saw the emergency Exit signs glowing and the trail of tiny floor lights leading up to them. I wanted to make a run for it. But what if the lobby's outer doors had been chained, too? And what if the lights came back on? I'd be cornered with no place to hide.

I tried to recall what scenery and props were in the wings, to think of something that might conceal me. I remembered the extension ladder. I could climb to the catwalk, then kick aside the ladder. I doubted Maggie would be able to get up the wall rungs, and, as far as I knew, she had no weapon.

I thought we had placed the ladder close to the center of the catwalk. Using the Exit signs to center myself, I moved slowly downstage, putting both hands out in front of me. I touched the ladder. Placing my foot lightly on the first rung, I reached with my left hand to pull myself up and gasped with pain. I had been too panicked to notice how badly my wrist was hurt. It was useless to me. I took a deep breath and quietly began to climb the ladder using only my right hand.

I heard Maggie at the bottom of the stairs to the stage. I continued on in slow motion. I heard her at the top of the steps, flicking switches. No lights came on. I continued to climb stealthily.

"Stay where you are," Maggie said loudly, as if she were directing campers.

Objects were knocked over. It sounded as if she was looking for something. There was a long moment of silence and I was afraid to move, afraid that just a shift of weight on the metal ladder would give me away. I figured I was little more than halfway up the thirty-foot climb.

A bright light came on. She had found a flashlight.

The light swung slowly over the stage, the beam wavering as if her hand was shaking, touching the ladder, passing below me. Maggie walked toward the apron of the stage. I watched the play of the beam along the rows of seats. It became steadier, then the light spun around and streaked up the ladder, stopping at me.

I scrambled up two rungs.

"Stop!" she commanded, shining the light in my eyes.

I felt as I did under the glare of stage lights. My stomach grew queasy. I began to sweat. I pulled myself up a rung, but my legs felt unsteady.

"One step farther and I will knock over the ladder," Maggie threatened.

I turned my face away from the light. "Why are you doing this to me?"

Maggie circled the ladder, trying to keep the beam in my eyes.

"Please tell me why."

"You still don't remember?" Her voice quivered. "You must! Every day of my life I wake up remembering the fire."

"The one Melanie was in?"

"You were only three when it occurred," she said, "the same age as Melanie, and your parents were careful not to talk about it. But the memory is with you. You're standing in the third-floor window with Liza. The lights of fire trucks and emergency vehicles are shining up at you. A crowd has gathered below."

As she spoke, a wave of sickness washed over me. I

gritted my teeth and took a step up. My hands were slippery with sweat.

"Every time you stand on a stage with lights shining up at you, darkened faces in the audience watching you, the memory and the fear come back."

I climbed another rung. My heart pounded in my ears.

I could feel the heat at my back. I saw strange faces three stories below me, people looking up from a dark New York street. There were lights in my eyes, a dizzying pattern of red, yellow, and blue lights on the street below.

"Jenny, come on! Jenny, please!" Liza begged. She reached for my hand, then grasped my fingers. The metal ladder that had inched toward us finally rested against the windowsill, but I didn't want to get on it. It clanked and moved with each step of the firefighter climbing toward us. "Don't be afraid. I'll help you."

"It's coming back, isn't it?" Maggie observed, her voice breaking through the memory.

There was no blue gleam in these images and no blue gleam in those I had seen at Maggie's house. I should have noticed that before. When I'd gazed at Melanie's picture, I had seen the fragments of buried memory, not the images of a psychic vision.

"Brian recognized you the first day of camp from a photo Liza had shown him," Maggie went on, "but he didn't tell me until this morning. He pretended interest in you so he could find out why you were here. It was stupid of him. I know why, and you, remembering as you must now, will understand why I had to kill Liza."

"I will never understand!"

"You will!" she shouted back. "And you'll remember every horrible detail and suffer as I have every day since the fire.

"We were neighbors in New York, all of us working long hours, raising small children. Your parents let Brian and Melanie stay with you, even when they hired a sitter. My husband was glad—it saved money—but I should have known better. Liza was a wild child. One February night, when I had Brian with me and had left Melanie with your baby-sitter, Liza played with matches."

I sagged against the ladder, guessing what came next.

"Liza set the fire. Liza killed Melanie!"

Now I understood what my sister had been referring to in her final e-mail, the terrible thing she had done but didn't mean to. "And when Liza saw you and Brian, she remembered it," I said.

"She remembered the fire, but she didn't recognize Brian or me. In New York she knew me as Mrs. Jones. When I divorced, I took back my maiden name. The name Brian Jones is common enough, and Brian is a man now, not a five-year-old boy. I didn't tell her who we were until the day before she died.

"For the first three weeks of camp I quietly watched her shine, dark-haired, blue-eyed, and pretty as my daughter would have been, a bright future ahead of her, the future my daughter should have had." Maggie's voice grew breathless. "Liza talked endlessly about her experiences—experiences that should have been Melanie's—about all her successes—successes my child deserved! "

Maggie turned suddenly. The beam of her flashlight dodged around the stage. "What's that? Who's there?"

"I didn't hear anything."

I figured that someone else was in the building, but if it was someone who wanted to hurt me, I was no worse off. And if it was someone who would help, then better to pretend I'd heard nothing. Maggie wasn't thinking clearly enough to question the cut in electric power; perhaps she thought I had done it.

The beam of her flashlight paused at a table of tools. Maggie walked over to it, and I took two more steps up.

"At the end of the third week someone set a fire in Drama House," Maggie continued as she fingered the sharp tools. "Liza could brag about her experience with fire, too—how she and her sister had escaped with their baby-sitter through a third-floor window, but a play-mate had hidden in a closet and died."

Maggie's face looked distorted, her jaw and the deep sockets of her eyes illuminated by the light she held over the table.

"How your parents showed you the fire exits at every theater and every place you stayed, how they taught you what to do. Like I was a bad parent!"

The beam of her flashlight bobbed and glittered off the knives on the table.

"Like it was my fault that Melanie died!"

She picked up a wood chisel, a four-inch point with a sturdy handle. I glanced upward. There were six more rungs to the catwalk, but just one more would allow me to reach up and grasp it.

"Your parents told Liza it was Melanie's fault for hiding when the baby-sitter called her." Maggie's voice kept rising. "They should have told Liza how wicked she was, how she killed someone, how she murdered my daughter!"

"Liza was only four years old," I protested. "She didn't understand the consequences."

"Liza took from me my greatest treasure!" Maggie cried out, then lowered her voice. "Last summer I took back. I wrote the note she thought Mike had sent. I knew Liza would slip out, even wait for him till I could be sure she and I were alone. Finally I had justice. Your parents and I were even, each left with one child. Then you came." She took a deep breath. "I liked you, Jenny. I felt . . . motherly toward you, when I didn't know who you were."

"We can work things out, Maggie," I said. "We can get help for you and me, for our families—"

"Don't you listen?" she exploded. "No one can help me! No one can end for me that night I watched you being helped down the ladder, watched you and Liza and the baby-sitter. I waited on the street, clutching Brian's little hand." Maggie's voice grew hysterical. "I watched and I waited for Melanie. I'm waiting still!"

The abrupt shift of the flashlight warned me. I pulled myself up one more rung, then felt the impact of her rushing against the ladder. I flung my hands upward, grasping the edge of the metal walk as the ladder was dragged out from beneath me. It crashed onto the stage.

"Flashlight, flashlight," Maggie called from below, like a small child calling a pet—or an adult totally unhinged. "Where are you, flashlight?"

High above her I dangled in darkness. My left hand was useless. I hung by my right. She found the light and shined it up at me. I pulled back my head to study the structure of the catwalk, a suspended strip of metal lace. My shadow flickered over it like a black moth.

"It's almost over, Jenny," Maggie said, her voice growing eerily soft. "Sooner or later, you will let go. Everyone lets go, except me."

There was a ridge along the catwalk's edge, the thin piece of metal my fingers grasped, then a large gap between that and a restraining bar. I knew I had to swing my legs onto the narrow walkway, but my right hand was slick with sweat. If I swung my body hard, my hand would slip off. I hung from one arm, looking down at Maggie.

"Sooner or later."

"Maggie, I'm begging you—"

I stopped midsentence. I had felt the catwalk vibrate. I grasped the metal harder, but my grip kept slipping. My hand rotated, my palm sliding past the thin ridge.

"Hold on, Jenny!"

Mike's voice. He must have climbed the wall rungs. His footsteps shook the catwalk.

The base of my fingers suddenly slid past the edge. I tried to tighten my grip, but felt the rim of the catwalk moving toward the tips of my fingers. I was hanging by the tips—I couldn't hold on. "Mike!"

A hand swooped down.

The theater went black.

I've fallen, I thought; I've blacked out. But Mike's

fingers were wrapped tightly around my wrist. Maggie had turned off the flashlight.

"Other hand! Give me your other hand, Jenny!"

"Where are you? I can't see."

"Here. Right above you."

"I can't grip with this hand. I hurt it."

"Hurt it where?"

"My wrist."

Mike's fingers groped for mine, then moved quickly and lightly past my injured wrist and halfway down my forearm. Now he gripped hard.

"I'm lying on my stomach," he said, "and have my feet hooked around the walk. I'm going to pull you up."

He tried, but it was impossible from that angle.

"I can swing my body, swing my feet," I told him, "if you hold on tight. Don't let go."

He grasped my arms so fiercely I knew I'd have bruises. I swung my legs and hips as if I were on a high bar, till I caught hold of the walk with my feet. With Mike's help I clambered up the rest of the way.

He pulled me close and wrapped his arms tightly around me. I couldn't stop shaking.

"You're okay, Jen. I've got you."

I clung to him, burrowing my head into his chest. He reached with one hand to touch my face, then quickly put his arm around me again, as if he had sensed my panic when he let go. Instead of his hand, he used his cheek to smooth mine.

"I'm not going to let anything happen to you."

"Where is she?" I whispered. "Where's Maggie?"

"Don't know," he answered quietly. "Stay still. Listen."

There was a long minute of silence, then a sudden banging noise.

"The door," I said. "She's at the door at the bottom of the steps. She can't get out that way. It's chained."

"Chained?"

"From the inside," I told him. "How did you get in?"

"I tried the doors, everything was locked, so I came through Walker's window."

"Did you cut the power?" I asked.

"No."

"Then someone else is in the building."

He was silent for a moment. "Brian?"

"I don't know."

"Stay here," Mike instructed and carefully disentangled himself from me. "I'll see what's up."

When he stood, I grabbed his ankle. "Oh, no, you don't. Not without me."

"It's safer here."

"It's safer two against one," I argued.

"It could be two against two."

"All the more reason." I reached for his hand, pulled myself up, then grasped the restraining bar.

We climbed down the wall rungs, then tiptoed to the steps and paused to listen.

"I want you to stay behind me," Mike whispered.

"No way."

"Don't be heroic, Jenny. We just want to get out."

"Heroic? I'm faster and don't want to get stuck behind you."

He swallowed a laugh, then pulled me back against

him. "If we get out of here alive, you've got a date for a race."

I wondered if he thought I was as brave as I pretended. "Did you leave Walker's door open?"

"That's what we're shooting for."

When we reached the bottom of the steps, we crept side by side down the hall. My ears strained to pick up movement. We had to be close to the turn, I thought, close to Walker's office. I prayed no one had shut and locked the door. Finally my hands touched the corner of the hall.

"Almost there," I whispered.

Just as we reached the office door, something fell, something in Maggie's office.

Mike pushed me from behind. "Go, Jen! Go!"

I rushed through Walker's office toward the open window. Mike shoved me through and I pulled him out after me. We sprang to our feet, ready to run, then heard commotion inside the building. Maggie screamed. The blinds in her window were flattened against the glass, as if something had crashed against them. Mike and I waited, holding on to each other, shivering.

After a long moment the shades swung inward ominously, the weight no longer pressing on them. They were pulled up and Arthur peered out. He opened the window, his face shining in the pale light, a dark streak on his cheek.

"I'm all finished," he announced.

Mike's arms tightened around me.

"All done. There's no reason to be afraid."

Mike walked backward, away from the building, pulling me with him.

"I won't hurt you. It was her I had to kill," Arthur said. "She took what was mine. She killed the girl and pretended to be me. You understand, don't you? The watch and the bridge, they were mine. It's not right to take a man's identity. I had to kill her to get myself back."

He rubbed his cheek as he spoke, then studied the blood that had come off on his fingers, sniffing it, rubbing one finger against another. I thought I was going to throw up.

Gazing at us again, Arthur appeared relaxed, almost cheerful, as if a huge burden had been lifted from his shoulders. "You run along and call the police," he said. "I'll turn the electricity back on."

nineteen

The campus security office was small and smelled of Chinese carryout. I sat on a bench between Mike and Tomas, my wrist packed in ice. Walker stood by a window with a noisy air conditioner, his arms folded over his chest, his eyes puffy and bloodshot. Paul crouched in the corner of the paneled office, leaning against the wall, like a person folded up on himself.

According to Tomas, Mike had returned to the Student Union not long after I left with the sandwich for Maggie. He asked Tomas where I was, then raced off to the theater. When time elapsed and he didn't return, Tomas told Walker he was worried. On their way to Stoddard, they met up with Paul. The three of them found us outside Maggie's window, just after Arthur told us to call the police.

While Walker called on his cell phone, Paul climbed through the window to talk to Arthur, whom he had befriended. Paul had suspected from the beginning that Liza's murderer was someone who knew her and had sought the custodian's help in drawing out the killer by haunting the theater. He'd never guessed that as much as Arthur was helping him, he was helping Arthur find the person who had "taken" Arthur's identity. The haunting had succeeded in unnerving Maggie, precipitating her arguments with Brian, arguments that revealed to the eavesdropping Arthur that Maggie was the murderer.

Paul confirmed for us that Maggie was dead. Maybe he wasn't into violence as much as he wanted everyone to think: it was he who threw up, not me.

The police did not allow anyone else to enter the building. But they wanted to interview all of us, which was why we were gathered at the security office. Arthur was being held separately for the FBI. He had cut the power and chained the doors, planning to kill Maggie that night, realizing too late that I had returned to the building. He explained carefully to the police and us that while he had "killed" Maggie, he had "murdered" only four people. In his deranged mind, Maggie's death was a form of justice, a way of erasing Liza's death from his list. Since Maggie's death "didn't count," he didn't need to kill her beneath a bridge.

The police were still seeking Brian. When security went to fetch him at the Student Union, he wasn't there. I kept telling myself that Brian didn't realize his mother had killed Liza till it was too late. If he had, he would never have told her who I was; he wouldn't have betrayed me like that.

But in my heart I knew otherwise. He had probed to find out what I remembered of the fire because he knew that the fire was his mother's motive for murder; he was trying to discover if I had pieced together the puzzle.

The door to the office opened and Brian walked in with a police officer. All of us looked up. None of us knew what to say.

Brian glanced around. "This is a happy-looking group."

"Where were you?" Walker asked. "I left you with our students. You were supposed to be in charge."

"I was in charge," Brian replied lightly, "until I went home. I had a few things to take care of."

He slipped his hands in his pockets and casually rested one shoulder against the wall, looking as relaxed as a guy waiting for his pizza order. It was as if none of this horrid situation shocked him. I wanted to tell him how sorry I was about his mother, but his coolness quelled my sympathy.

Mike spoke up suddenly: "What did you do with the boat?"

"What boat?" Brian replied.

"The rowboat your mother signed out the day Liza was killed."

"I don't know what you're talking about."

"I think you do," Mike countered. "When Jenny told me Liza had been murdered beneath the pavilion, I wondered how her body could have been transported to the bridge without leaving a trail of blood. Then I realized that if a boat was floated in the shallow water close to the pavilion, a body could be carried out to it, even dragged. The blood left behind would be washed out by the tide. The boat, of course, would be stained."

A small smile curled the corners of Brian's mouth.

"I remembered that just before Liza died your mother had asked me how to sign out a boat from the college. During the movie tonight I met my friend who runs the boathouse. We checked the records as well as every boat in the yard and on the docks. The boat your mother signed out had been signed in by someone, but it was missing, probably has been since that night, which leads me to ask—where did you sink it?"

Brian shrugged his shoulders and spread his hands. "I have no idea what you're talking about."

The local police officer who had escorted Brian and had been listening attentively to our conversation cocked his head.

"What about Liza's bracelet?" I asked. "You urged me to search Paul's room. Did you plant it there? You had time when you returned our lunch trays."

He smiled but said nothing.

"And the fire alarm," I added.

"I'll take credit for that," Brian said agreeably.

Our conversation was interrupted by the arrival of a state trooper.

"Here's your ride," the local officer said to Brian. "I don't know what kind of games you're playing, Mr. Jones, but I suggest you don't play too hard till you meet with a lawyer. You told police that your mother came to you after the murder, and you helped her transport the body by boat. As for the fire alarm, we know who set it off, a local juvenile, not you."

"Just having a little fun with my friends," Brian replied, smiling. Then he turned to me, his eyes alight with amusement. "You look so amazed, Jenny. I told you at the beginning, I'm a better actor than Walker thinks." He flicked a glance at Walker. "Much better. Come visit me in L.A."

A campus security guard brought me back from Easton Hospital at two A.M. with my wrist in a cast and sling. The door to Drama House was open and I let myself in. Walker emerged from the common room, greeted me, then eyed the cast.

"Broken?"

"Yup."

He took a deep breath and let it out slowly. He looked exhausted, and his eyes, which had cleared before I left campus, had become red and puffy again.

"I'm sorry, Jenny."

"I'm sorry, too. Maggie was a very good friend to you."

He nodded, pressing his lips together several times before he could speak. "Your parents are on their way home from London. They caught the early flight out and will be here around one P.M. our time. I've contacted everyone else's parents and told them I'm closing camp." He gestured toward the doorway of the common room. "Everyone is upset. I told those who didn't want to sleep in their own rooms to bring a pillow and blanket here. The kids saved a sofa for you, but sleep wherever you can get comfortable. Did the doctor give you some painkillers?"

"Yes."

He followed me into the common room and sat in a chair with three cups of coffee next to it, where I guessed he was spending the night. Mike, Tomas, and Shawna were asleep on the floor in front of an empty sofa. Paul was sleeping in the corner of the room, curled on his side, his knees drawn up. Keri lay a few feet away from him.

I carefully stepped around the various sleepers till I reached Mike, then knelt and touched his cheek. "Thank you," I said softly, though I knew he didn't hear me.

Turning toward Tomas, I smiled when I saw he was sleeping with his backpack, one of his sketchbooks on top. I took it and returned to Walker.

"I'm going to my room."

"Good girl," he replied, as if I were a child. "You'll rest better there."

"Would you let Tomas know I have one of his books?"

Walker nodded. We said good night and I went straight to my room.

Without turning on the lights, I closed the door behind me and carried the sketchpad over to the window seat. Making myself comfortable there, I opened the book and studied Tomas's newest drawings, dark silky pencil lines on moon-bright pages, sketches of the bridge, the gazebo, and the pavilion. I closed my eyes and let my mind wander. The scenes Tomas had drawn slowly evolved into real scenes, a stretch of tall grass, the concrete bridge, dark wood pilings, the wide creek. A blue gleam surrounded the images, but I felt no fear. The breeze was gentle and the creek lapped peacefully.

"I know you are here," I whispered to my sister. "You'll always be with me in my heart. But sleep now, Liza. Sweet dreams now. Sweet dreams only for you and me."

twenty

Shawna awakened me at noon the next day, telling me my parents had phoned from the airport near Baltimore and would soon be in Wisteria. Most of the other kids had already been picked up by nervous family members, but she had put off her departure so we could say goodbye.

Tomas stopped in after her.

"I've got your sketchpad," I told him.

"I came for a hug," he replied. "You scared me, Jenny."

Before I got a chance to see Mike, my parents arrived and asked me to go down to the creek with them. We spent an hour at the pavilion, standing on the deck, gazing out at the water. We talked about Liza, remembering, laughing, and crying some.

"Well, dearest," my father said, resting his hand on mine, "we should get back to campus. Your mother and

I spoke to Walker when we arrived and asked him to join us for an early tea."

"You did?" I replied, surprised. "You met with him and it went okay?"

"Of course," my father said, "we're grown men."

My mother rolled her eyes. "It was as awkward as two old bachelors meeting at their former girlfriend's wedding. I'm the one who proposed tea, and neither your father nor Walker had the nerve to say no."

I laughed and strolled down the ramp with them. When we reached the bottom, I saw Mike standing by the tall grasses that surrounded the pavilion, a dark-haired man next to him. They turned toward us at the same time, the man closing a small black book.

"Hi, Mike. I want you to meet my parents."

My mother quickly patted her blowing curls into place, her hands making little butterfly motions.

The man introduced himself as the Reverend James Wilcox. He had Mike's blue eyes, broad shoulders, and deep voice.

"We were just praying for Liza," Reverend Wilcox said.

I was amused by the way he and my father studied each other. Both knew how to assume a commanding, theatrical presence—and they were giving it their best effort. Mike examined my cast, but we said little, letting our parents do the talking. Then my father, playing one of his favorite roles—famous actor acknowledging an apprentice—asked Mike about his interest in theater.

"I like it okay," Mike replied, "but the real reason I came to camp was to live away from home."

"What?" I exclaimed softly.

The reverend's jaw dropped. "I don't think I heard you right, Michael."

"Well, drama is fun. I'm just not as interested in it as I used to be."

"I can't believe it." The reverend blinked a couple times and his voice resonated with incredulity. "I truly cannot believe it!"

I stifled a smile. Mike's father was as pompous and melodramatic as mine.

Reverend Wilcox turned to my parents. "I have been praying for the last two years that I would accept my son's calling. There is, after all, something blessed in every gift."

"Indeed," said my father.

"I have spent the last two weeks reading Michael's college catalog and the drama books he left behind. And now, just as I near acceptance, he tells me he's not interested."

"Tragic," my father replied.

"Excuse me," I said, "I'd like to talk to Mike alone. Mom and Dad, why don't you take Reverend Wilcox to tea with you and Walker?"

Ministers ought to be good at reconciliation, I thought.

My father looked at me, puzzled. "Aren't you coming, dearest? I had so hoped—"

My mother, having better instincts than he, shook her head at him, then steered him and Mike's father toward Goose Lane.

When our parents were well out of earshot, I turned to Mike. "What was that all about?"

He ignored my question. "How are you feeling, Jenny?"

"Apparently, better than you," I said, and took a step closer.

He took a step back. "I'm fine."

"Except for your minor surgery last night—did you undergo a brain transplant?"

He smiled a little and started walking toward the docks, striding quickly, as if he couldn't stand still and look at me. "No, but I had a lot of dreams—actually the same one over and over."

I struggled to keep up with him.

"I kept searching for you in a dark theater," he said. "I'd find you, but each time I reached for you, you'd slip through my fingers."

"And after that nightmare you decided that you didn't like working in theaters anymore. I get it. Hey, slow down! And look at me, please." I grabbed the edge of his shirt. "You're making it difficult for a one-armed girl."

He stopped. "Sorry."

"Look me in the eye, Mike, and tell me you don't love theater."

He gazed at my hair instead.

"Lower," I told him.

"Your hair is like a burning bush."

"Lower," I repeated, then caught my breath when his eyes met mine.

"All right," I said. "You had no trouble looking in my eyes and saying all those romantic lines during auditions. Let's see how well you can act now. Eyeball to eyeball, tell me you don't love theater."

"I wasn't acting then."

"Mike, I know what you're afraid of. You think that I'll think you're trying to score points with— What did you say?"

"I wasn't acting, Jenny. I didn't hang around Liza hoping to meet her father, but hoping to meet her sister."

"Me?" My heart did a somersault.

"Liza kept talking about you, what you did, what you said, what you thought, how you could make her laugh. She showed me pictures of you. I kept waiting for you to come see her."

"I can't believe it!"

"I realized too late that Liza mistook my interest in you for interest in her. I felt terrible about it, but I didn't tell her the truth because I didn't want to hurt her. I tried to back out, but she wouldn't let go. In the end I think she began to figure it out. The morning she died, she gave me the picture of the two of you."

I closed my eyes and swallowed hard.

"When I learned from Keri that Liza had been lured out of the house by a note she thought I wrote, I felt responsible for her death. If I hadn't been so eager to meet you, if I hadn't hung around so much, she might not have fallen for it."

I shook my head. "You're not responsible, Mike. If it wasn't that, it would have been something else," I said. "Maggie was in so much pain, she would have figured a way to get her no matter what."

"Because of the note I thought that the murderer was someone who knew Liza," he continued. "But when the police decided it was a serial killer, I was so relieved I accepted the theory. I convinced myself that Keri had made up the story—or maybe wrote the note herself—to prove to Paul that Liza didn't like him.

"I didn't want to come back this year, but Walker kept calling me. I decided that to get past what had happened, I had to return. When I arrived I went straight to the theater, because that's where Liza was happiest. I was shocked to see a girl onstage delivering lines exactly as Liza had. I suspected it was you, and when I met you beneath the bridge, I knew for sure."

Mike and I had reached the docks and walked out on one. I followed him down a ramp and onto a floating platform.

"I couldn't understand why you had come, Jenny, or why, after all that had happened I still wanted so badly to know you. I felt wrong for feeling the way I did, and I tried to avoid you, but it was impossible. You weren't a dream girl but a real girl, and the more I got to know you the harder it was to stop thinking of you."

As he spoke he kept his distance, letting only his eyes touch me. His eyes alone were enough to make me feel unsteady on my feet.

"Mike, sometimes when I look at you it's like—" I hesitated, trying to find the words. Now I knew why people quoted plays and poems. "It feels like the ground is moving beneath me."

He laughed. "It is, Jenny. We're standing on a floating dock."

"That's not what I meant."

The words "I love you" were still too new, too scary,

but somehow I had to explain to him. "I think there should be no more accidents."

He studied me a moment, his eyes turning gray. "Sure, that's okay, I understand."

"No! Wait! You don't understand. I meant that from now on every kiss of mine is purely intentional."

"Is it?"

I waited for him to take me in his arms, to sweep me off my feet, as dramatic types are supposed to do. He didn't move.

"So, uh, don't you want to kiss me?"

"You go first," he replied. "I did last time."

But I suddenly felt shy.

"If you want to kiss me, Jenny, why don't you?"

I held on to his arm with one hand, stood on my toes, and kissed him on the cheek. It was horribly awkward.

Then Mike leaned down and gently kissed the fingers of my injured hand. He kissed each bruise on my arms, the places he had gripped to keep me from falling. He drew me close to him and cupped my head with one hand, laying his cheek against mine.

"I'll never stop wanting to kiss you," he whispered, then sealed his words with tenderness.

about the author

$\mathcal{A}$ former high school and college teacher with a Ph.D. in English literature from the University of Rochester, ELIZABETH CHANDLER now writes full time and enjoys visiting schools to talk about the process of creating books. She has written numerous picture books for children under her real name, Mary Claire Helldorfer, as well as romances for teens under her pen name, Elizabeth Chandler. Her novels include the trilogy *Kissed by an Angel; Dark Secrets: Legacy of Lies;* and *Dark Secrets: Don't Tell,* published by Archway Paperbacks.

When not writing, Mary Claire enjoys biking, gardening, watching sports, and daydreaming. She has been a die-hard Orioles fan since she was a kid and a daydreamer for just as long. Mary Claire lives in Baltimore with her husband, Bob, and their cat, Puck.

DARK SECRETS™

by Elizabeth Chandler

#1: Legacy of Lies

#2: Don't Tell

#3: No Time to Die

Archway Paperbacks
Published by Pocket Books

3027-01

William Corlett's

THE MAGICIAN'S HOUSE QUARTET

Thirteen-year-old William Constant and his two younger sisters, Mary and Alice, have come to ancient, mysterious Golden House in Wales for the holidays. Their lives will never be the same once they enter the Magician's House—and discover their destiny.

THE STEPS UP THE CHIMNEY

THE DOOR IN THE TREE

THE TUNNEL BEHIND THE WATERFALL

THE BRIDGE IN THE CLOUDS

Available from Archway Paperbacks
Published by Pocket Books

3044-01

Todd Strasser's

HERE COMES HEAVENLY

Here Comes Heavenly

She just appeared out of nowhere. Spiky purple hair, tons of earrings and rings. Hoops through her eyebrow and nostril, and tattoos on both arms. She said her name was Heavenly Litebody. Our nanny. Nanny???

Dance Magic

Heavenly is cool and punk. She sure isn't the nanny our parents wanted for my baby brother, Tyler. And what's with all those ladybugs?

Pastabilities

Heavenly Litebody goes to Italy with the family and causes all kinds of merriment! But...is the land of *amore* ready for her?

Spell Danger

Kit has to find a way to keep Heavenly Litebody, the Rands' magical, mysterious nanny from leaving the family forever.

Available from Archway Paperbacks
Published by Pocket Books

2307.01